A LIFE IN HER HANDS

A LIFE
IN HER HANDS

SHIRLEE EVANS

HERALD PRESS
Scottdale, Pennsylvania
Kitchener, Ontario
1987

Library of Congress Cataloging-in-Publication Data

Evans, Shirlee, 1931-
   A life in her hands.

   Summary: When she discovers that she is pregnant,
fifteen-year-old Gail is torn by indecision about
whether to keep the baby as she would like or give it up for adoption.
   [1. Unmarried mothers—Fiction.   2. Pregnancy—
Fiction.   3. Christian life—Fiction]   I. Title.
PZ.E8925Li   1987   [Fic]   87-8779
ISBN 0-8361-3441-9 (pbk.)

A LIFE IN HER HANDS
Copyright © 1987 by Herald Press, Scottdale, Pa. 15683
   Published simultaneously in Canada by Herald Press,
   Kitchener, Ont. N2G 4M5. All rights reserved.
Library of Congress Catalog Card Number: 87-8779
International Standard Book Number: 0-8361-3441-9
Printed in the United States of America
Cover art by Sibyl Graber Gerig
Design by David Hiebert

92 91 90 89 88 87 10 9 8 7 6 5 4 3 2 1

*To
Vera Lee*

Contents

1

Pregnant!

Gail hugged the heavy green sweater tight around her as the October breeze rippled her gray skirt. A wind gust scattered the dry leaves under an aging elm where she stood—a tree just like the many lining the quiet street. It was turning cooler.

She rolled a crisp leaf into brown fragments under her toe as she waited alone that Friday afternoon, leaning back against the cold cement fence bordering the yard of an old long-vacant house.

Kids from her high school passed by in groups without a word or even a glance in her direction, chattering and laughing, as they hurried home. It was as though she didn't exist. Gail sighed. She supposed she didn't . . . to them. She usually walked home with Lorna. Today she had stayed behind to talk to Steve.

Gail kept her head down, her shoulder length chestnut hair falling forward, veiling her face as she flaked the decaying leaf into shreds under her shoe. At last she became aware someone had stopped in front of her.

"What's the idea stuffing a note in my locker asking me to meet you here?" a male voice questioned.

Slowly Gail raised her head, her hair falling back to reveal an oval face, large brown eyes, and full lips. It would have been a pretty face if it had not had such long practice masking feelings behind dark expressionless eyes. Life was easier, Gail had found, when others overlooked her existence.

"I needed to see you," she spoke.

"It's a wonder I found it—the note I mean," the tall blond youth remarked with an impatient sigh. "What'd you do, shove it through the vent in my locker?" He wore jeans topped by a blue nylon windbreaker.

Gail nodded.

"I told you I couldn't see you this weekend," Steve protested.

"I know. But it was important."

He shifted his lanky frame from one leg to the other, glancing up the street. It was empty except for a chipmunk skittering up a tree. "Do you want to walk?" he asked.

"I'd just as soon stay here. Most of the kids have gone home."

"Okay," Steve said with a shrug, turning to lift himself to sit atop the three-foot high cement fence.

Gail looked up into his face. He was the first boy she had ever loved. Sometimes she was certain he loved her. "Steve, I've got a problem. I mean . . . we have a problem."

"I've got no problems," he noted with a grin.

"I'm afraid you do. It's called a baby."

His expression froze as he stared down at her. "A what?"

"You're going to be a father," she added in a thin-pinched voice.

"You must be crazy!" Steve's long face, with its fading summer tan, whitened. "Are you saying you're ... that you're...."

"Pregnant," she asserted, adding the word he could not seem to speak.

He continued to stare at her, his hands gripping the cold cement on either side of him. "Pregnant! You're pregnant?" He glanced up, as though afraid someone had heard. There was no one in sight, not even the chipmunk. "Gail, you can't do this to me," he whispered huskily.

She felt numbed. Empty. Her fantasy—of Steve encircling her in his arms, taking care of her—was not to be. She turned away, tears edging her dark eyes. She had felt alone many times during her fifteen years, but never quite so alone as at this moment.

At last Steve lowered himself from the fence. He reached out, touching her shoulder with his fingertips. "I'm sorry. It's just that—I mean—coming out like this without warning, hitting me square between the eyes.... It's hard to take in."

She turned back. "Yeah. I didn't know of a better way."

He drew a deep breath, shoved his hands into the pockets of his windbreaker, then looked up through the withering leaves that still clung to the tree limbs. "Gail, I intend to be a doctor. My dad's a doctor. I have no excuse for acting dumb about this. It's just that—well, it scares me."

"Me, too," she responded. "And don't ask if I'm sure, because I am. I bought one of those kits at the drug store to test myself at home. It came up positive."

"How far along do you think you are?" he questioned.

"About three months."

"Three months! Gail, are you nuts? You should have guessed a long time ago. If you keep waiting it will be too late to do anything about it."

She glared at him. "Like what? An abortion?"

He nodded. "What'd you have in mind? You don't expect us to get married do you? I'm only seventeen. You're fifteen. We're too young to think of marriage. And, as I've told you before, I've got...."

"Yes, yes, I know," she interrupted. "You've got years of schooling ahead so you can become a doctor just like your dear old daddy!"

"What's wrong with that?" Steve demanded. "You don't need to sound so sarcastic."

"What kind of doctor are you going to be if you can't take responsibility right now for what you've done? For what *we've* done," she retorted, surprised at her own outburst.

Steve stared at her, taken back by Gail's sudden assertiveness. They stood there on the deserted street corner facing each other, anger and fear tearing at them both. Finally, without a word, Steve reached out, pulling her to him. She stiffened, then relaxed, burying her face against the crisp nylon of his jacket.

"We'll work it out somehow, Gail. We'll find a way to make things come out all right." He took her hand and began pulling her along. "Come on. Let's walk. I've got to move. Do something. I can't just stand here."

Gail's tenseness eased. She realized the news had been a shock to Steve. He would help her now—stand by her. Everything would be all right again. She was not alone any longer.

They walked in silence for a time. At last Steve spoke. "What do you want to do? You aren't thinking we should get married, are you?"

"I don't know," she answered with a tired shrug.

"The way I see it there are only two choices. It's either an abortion or wait until the baby's born and then put it out for adoption. You must have thought about it. What do you want to do?"

"I don't want a big fat stomach," Gail replied. "If we can't get married, then I don't want to be pregnant."

"So you did expect me to marry you."

Gail continued looking down as they walked, absentmindedly avoiding the cracks in the sidewalk. In a few months she would not be able to see her feet when she walked. Not if she remained pregnant another six months. "I thought you might *want* to marry me," she ventured at last. "For your baby, at least."

"Good grief, Gail. I've got another seven months of high school. In seven months the baby will be...." He hesitated. "The baby will be a month old in seven months. Then there's still...."

"I know. I know," she interrupted again. "There's still college and medical school and all that stuff. You've told me often enough."

"It may not seem important to you, but it is to me and my folks," Steve reminded her. "It's my whole future."

"And what about *my* future? What about our baby's future?" she asked.

"Gail." Steve stopped, turning her to face him. "At this moment it's only a fetus. It's not a baby. It's not even human—just a mass of cells."

"It's the beginning of a baby. It's the way you and I began," she protested, placing a hand on her still-flat stomach. "When does it become a baby?"

He shook his head. "I don't know. People have different ideas about it. Some say at conception. Others think it's when the mother feels the baby move, and still others say it's not until after it's born."

"You just called it a baby," Gail reminded.

"Oh, come on. You're not making this any easier." Steve turned and started on.

Fright gripped her as she watched him walk away. "Wait, Steve!" she called, running to catch up. "You said it sounded as though I expected you to marry me. Well, it sounds to me like you expect me to have an abortion."

He nodded without looking at her. "That's what I think."

"Abortion frightens me," Gail told him. "I don't know that much about it."

"Okay," Steve said, stopping again. "Look, there's a bench over there. Let's sit down and try to make some sensible decisions. We've got to quit arguing."

She followed him to the bench. Suddenly Steve seemed much younger, like a lost little boy.

They sat down and he turned to her. "First of all, I can't marry you. It wouldn't work even if I quit school and found a job. I'm going to be a doctor, Gail. I won't be able to marry anyone for years. As far as I'm concerned marriage is completely out for us. That leaves just the other two choices."

She glanced away. "I don't want to have a baby and then give it away to strangers. And I don't want to look pregnant so everyone in the whole world knows."

"You wouldn't have to stay around here," Steve said. "They have places where girls like you can go until after their babies are born. No one would have to know."

She glanced at him. His words, *girls like you*, sickened her. "I'd know. So would you. We'd always know that out there somewhere we had a son or a daughter. We'd know until the day we died."

"So have an abortion then."

"We'd still know, Steve. We'd always wonder what we had killed. We'd know!" Tears escaped Gail's eyes.

"That brings us right back to adoption," Steve said matter-of-factly.

She wiped her flushed cheeks with the back of a hand.

14

"I always thought I was adopted. I don't look like my mom, my dad, or my brother. Dad left us when I was a baby. Mom never cared as much about me as she did my brother Aaron. As for my father ... I honestly think he hates me. The only times I saw him was when he stopped by to pick Aaron up for a weekend. He never once asked me to go with them."

"You've never talked about your family," Steve remarked. "All I've known was that you came to stay with the Grants when they decided to take in a foster daughter."

"I don't even like thinking about my family. I was taken away from my mother when I was thirteen. She's alcoholic. The Grants are the third family I've lived with."

Sympathy touched Steve's eyes. "I didn't realize your life had been that rough. I'm really sorry. And now this happens to you."

"It's happening to *us*, Steve. "To both of us."

He smiled slightly and nodded, reaching out to push a strand of brown hair back from her face. "So you really think you were adopted?"

"I'm the only one in our family with brown eyes," she noted.

"That happens in a lot of familes."

"Yeah, I guess." She felt tired. Her stomach was growing queasy again. She tried ignoring it as she straightened her shoulders. "I couldn't stand being responsible for a child ending up in a situation where it wasn't loved. I know what it's like, when your parents don't want you."

"Does that mean you'd rather have an abortion?" Steve asked.

Gail sat for a time before speaking. "I don't know. Maybe that is what I'm saying. I can't make that decision right now."

"You've got to soon," Steve told her. "Look, if you're going to have an abortion it has to be done right away. We don't have weeks to think things over. You're right at that time now, if I remember the health seminar we had on abortion last year, when it's almost too late to do it the easy way."

Gail shuddered. "Easy way! Steve, do you think our baby can hear us talking about it like this?"

"Now you're being stupid. Look," his voice softened, "let's both go home and talk to our parents. They've got to know. You can talk to Mrs. Grant, can't you? You told me you get along with her."

"Yes, I guess. Sue's been nice. Mr. Grant—Mack—has been okay too. I don't know how he will feel about me, though, after he hears about this. As for Ginger, she hates me anyway."

"Ginger's not all that bad," Steve said, rising to the defense of Gail's sixteen-year-old red-haired foster sister. "She didn't used to be such a loud mouth. You two didn't hit it off right in the beginning, that's all. She was looking forward to having a foster sister before you came to live with them."

"She never acted like it," Gail commented.

"That's because you never gave her a chance. Ginger wanted someone to hang around with. Someone to do girl-type stuff with. All you did that first month was go to school or hide away in your room. At least that's what Ginger said."

"People like Ginger bother me," Gail said. "She comes on too strong. She was mad, I think, when we started dating."

Steve laughed. "We've gone to the same schools since first grade. We went to a couple games together in junior high, but there was never anything between us. To tell the truth, she comes on too strong for me, too. Maybe that's why you and I hit it off so well. We're the soft silent types."

Gail watched Steve as he talked, her large eyes hiding the fright locked inside. "I don't feel soft right now. But I do wish I could keep silent. I don't want to have to tell the Grants. It's been bad enough telling you. But guess I have to."

"Come on." Steve was pulling her to her feet. "There's a bus coming. It'll stop if we stay here."

They started back to the corner where Gail had waited for him earlier.

"Are you going to tell the Grants tonight?"

"I'll tell Sue. Are you telling your parents when you get home?"

Steve nodded. "Dad's out of town for the weekend. But I'll talk to Mom."

Gail searched his face. "Will you call me later? At least sometime this weekend?"

"Sure." He turned away. "Be seeing you."

"Steve...."

He stopped without turning around.

Gail hesitated. She needed more reassurance from him, something to hang onto to help her through the evening. But he simply stood there with his back to her. She sighed. "Never mind. Good luck."

"Yeah. You, too." A couple more steps and he turned the corner and was gone.

If only he had kissed her, held her, done or said something to let her know he cared. She was the mother of his ... fetus. She could almost hear him correcting her thoughts for starting to use the word baby.

Mother! That word, too, caught in her mind. She was a mother, whether she allowed the baby to grow inside her, or stopped its development with an abortion. She was still, would always be, its mother. Gail's mind took off in a wild race. A mother was supposed to be strong and wise—all the things she was not. Just like her own mother who had never measured up. How could she mother a child when she herself had so much growing up to do?

Gail walked slowly home. The high school was only six blocks from where she lived with the Grants. She wished it were twenty. How would she tell Sue? They were probably wondering what had happened to her. Gail glanced at her watch. Sue no doubt had been home for several hours from the convalescent center where she worked. She usually had dinner ready so they could all sit down together by six. It was already six-thirty. Mack would be there. And, of course, there was always Ginger.

Sue was the only member of the Grant family Gail had come to feel at ease with in the seven months she had lived with them. Mack was full of energy like his daughter Ginger. They both had red hair, although of different hues. Father and daughter joked and teased each other unmercifully. Since Gail was not used to that kind of closeness with her own father, she found it difficult to know how to react around Mack and Ginger. Sue seemed to sense Gail's timidity, paying special attention to the girl whenever father and daughter were in one of their roughhouse moods.

Church meant a lot to Mack and Sue. Ginger had attended church and Sunday school all her life. She knew all the songs when there were no books to use, and where to locate Bible verses with just the flip of a page. Gail felt uncomfortable and just plain dumb at those times.

Gail was expected to attend Sunday morning worship service with the Grants. Beyond that she was not made to go to any of the other church activities. Gail went to church on Sunday mornings and that was all.

Pastor Wilkes seemed nice, although she really didn't

know him. He was rather heavyset with curly white hair. He was Gail's fantasy of what a grandfather should look like. But it was only a fantasy, for she had never known her own grandparents for reasons she didn't understand.

Gail figured church was probably all right for some people. She just wasn't used to it. She didn't understand the terms Pastor Wilkes used and cared nothing about learning. It finally became a habit to sit through the entire service without hearing a word of what was said. After all, she had other things on her mind these days.

She wondered if Mack and Sue's religious beliefs would now cause her problems. Gail knew some people looked on sex as wrong if you weren't married. She supposed church people had always been a little behind the times. People talked about it the way they talked about anything else. Being pregnant was different though. You were supposed to know enough not to get pregnant if you didn't want a baby.

Gail hesitated when she reached the two-story white frame house before going in. She finally turned the knob on the front door and pushed it open.

"I'm home. Sorry I'm late," she called out in what she hoped was a normal-sounding voice.

2

Life's Thin Line

"I was wondering what happened to you," Sue remarked as Gail closed the door behind her. An open stairway leading to the upstairs bedrooms stood before Gail. To her right was the living area. A family room and kitchen were out of sight just beyond the dining room where Sue, Mack, and Ginger now sat at the table within view of the front door. "You've never been this late before," Sue said.

"I ran into Steve after school. We got to talking. I didn't realize how late it was."

Ginger, in a faded orange sweat shirt that intensified the auburn hue of her hair, glanced up, a fork poised in midair. "What's the matter? Forget how to tell time?" she asked, her freckled face shadowed by thick fluffy waves.

Her father's freckle-blotched complexion was less pronounced, his hair of a lighter shade flecked with white. Mack was husky, but far from stout. Although normally radiating a cheerfulness not easily turned off, he now cautioned his daughter with a frown. "Come on," he said, motioning Gail toward her empty chair. "You'd better hurry or it will all be gone. Everyone's entitled to forget the time once every seven months or so."

"I'm not hungry. Guess I spoiled my appetite with that milk shake Steve bought for me," Gail lied. "I don't feel so great right now." She didn't have to lie about that at least! "Is it all right if I go to my room and lie down?"

Sue got up from the table and came in to where Gail stood by the front door. Sue was an attractive woman, whether dressed in denim or silk. Today she wore tailored navy pants and a soft pink blouse. She placed a hand on Gail's forehead. "You're not feverish. Maybe if you ate you'd feel better."

"I couldn't swallow a thing. Honest."

Sue cocked her head to one side, her hazel eyes reflecting her smile. Short fawn-shaded hair lay in wispy waves swept up and back behind her ears. "All right. Go lie down. I'll bring you something later."

Gail started up the stairs as Sue went back to the table.

"Why do you baby her?" Ginger questioned, the words following Gail up to the second floor. "You never let me get away with things like that."

Reaching her bedroom, Gail went in and closed the door, sealing Ginger's words and the world out. She was tired. Pulling off her sweater, she tossed it on the bed and sat down with a sigh. She just hoped Sue would be as understanding later, when she told her foster mother about the baby.

The Grants had been good to her. If it weren't for Ginger this would have been the best of her three foster homes. But things between the two girls had been strained from the very beginning. Since then their relationship had been going even further downgrade. She still felt Ginger was probably jealous because of Steve.

The thought brought a smile to Gail's tight-set lips. No one had ever before been jealous of her that she could remember. Maybe she had sort of lorded it over Ginger.

This was a new section of town to Gail, with a new school. She had come to the Grants hoping to change her image, make new friends, and be somebody for a change. Sue had taken her shopping that first weekend, helping her choose clothes that looked especially nice on her. Sue then made an appointment with her own hairdresser where Gail's long fine hair was cut to cascade softly to her shoulders and around her face. The new clothes and hairstyle, however, had done nothing to heal the scars the girl carried. Except for Steve and Lorna, her one and only close girl friend, Gail was as much of a loner and outsider as before.

She lay back on the bed looking around the room. It had been the Grants' spare bedroom before she came. Sue had redecorated it in lavender just for her. At first Ginger tried to be friendly, in a rather grudging way. But Gail never felt a part of their family. As she thought about it she realized she had never belonged much of anywhere.

When Sue came to Gail's room later with hot herb tea and a plate of reheated food, she found the girl standing at the window looking down on the darkening street.

"Feeling better?" Sue asked, placing the tray she carried on the small study desk.

"A little." Gail went to the desk, sitting on the low-backed chair. "Sue, I need to talk to you."

The woman sat on the edge of the bed. "All right," she said.

Gail picked up the cup of hot fragrant tea and sipped it. The liquid soothed her tightening throat. "I didn't just happen to run into Steve today. I asked him to meet me after school. I told him...." She stopped and took a breath, shakily replacing the cup on the tray. "I told him I'm pregnant."

Gail waited for a reaction from the woman. There was none.

"It's Steve's baby," Gail added. "I'm about three months—that way."

Sue got to her feet, crossing to where Gail sat staring at the wall in front of her, as still as stone. "Oh, honey." She put an arm around the girl's shoulder, pulling Gail close. "I'm so sorry. No wonder you've been so quiet lately. You must be terribly frightened."

Tears streaked Gail's face as Sue's sympathetic tone melted her forced calm. "I thought you'd be mad. I've been so scared. So afraid you and Mack would kick me out of your family."

"We don't kick people who are down and hurting." She knelt beside Gail's chair looking into the girl's pale face, her brown eyes appearing even darker. "Did Steve have any idea a baby was on the way before today?"

Gail shook her head. She told Sue of the things she and Steve had talked about, adding, "Since you're more of a mother to me that my own mother has ever been, I wanted to tell you first."

Getting to her feet, Sue stepped back to sit on the bed again. She leaned forward thoughtfully. "There isn't going to be any easy solution," the woman spoke at last. "Steve's right about one thing—a decision has to be made as soon as possible."

Feeling the need to plead for understanding, Gail made a try for sympathy. "Steve is the only boy I've ever dated or been this close to. No boy ever cared about me before. I love him. We were wrong in not being careful. I know that. But, Sue, sex isn't wrong when two people *really* love each other."

Sue's eyes evidenced a seriousness belying her smile.

"Many people today believe casual sex is all right, whether they're in love or not. But, Gail, God didn't intend sex to be abused. Sex is his gift, to be enjoyed by husbands and wives within their marriage. Outside of marriage sex is only an artificial thrill. A substitute for mature love and commitment. An experience that never quite satisfies."

Sue stopped, took a breath, then shook her head. "I didn't mean to get so carried away. Right now we need to face the situation and decide what to do about this tiny life that's already started to develop."

Gail breathed easier. She had braced herself for a lecture. Now it was behind her. Sue, she reasoned, just didn't understand the concept of love in the modern world.

"I'll make an appointment with our family doctor tomorrow morning," Sue was saying. "We need to make sure your suspicions are correct."

"Oh, it's there all right," Gail said, patting her stomach.

"We'll have to talk to Steve's family, too," Sue added. "Steve and Ginger have attended the same schools since first grade. But as families we tend to run in different circles. I know Mrs. Miller a little better than I know Dr. Miller. I'm afraid she'll fight to the death anyone standing in the way of Steve becoming a doctor. He's their only child. It's a matter of pride with her."

"Then you really believe marriage is out for Steve and me?" Gail questioned.

"As long as Steve doesn't want to marry you, I can't foresee his parents, at least his mother, encouraging that to happen."

"Which leaves just adoption or abortion," Gail commented dryly. "I don't like either of those choices. As I told Steve today, I've always thought I was adopted. My parents never cared about me. Not ever. I've never really belonged anywhere. You and Mack have been good to me, but I'm not your real daughter. Not like Ginger."

There was a sadness behind Sue's eyes as she listened. "Most families who adopt love their children. There are so many abortions now it's getting harder and harder for childless couples to adopt."

Gail could feel Sue's warmth and love. This was the kind of mother she hoped she would be someday. "You believe I should go ahead and have the baby then, and give it away."

"Yes," Sue replied. "But you must make up your own mind. I just wish you didn't have such a distorted view of adoption. I know it's not a perfect solution. I'm sure a mother always wonders about her child after giving it up. But Gail, abortion is not the easy way out it's sometimes pictured. You will still think about your baby. Only after an abortion you'd never be able to wonder where your son or daughter was or what he or she had become."

"Would you hate me if I had an abortion?" Gail asked.

"No. I wouldn't hate you. But to me abortion is just a nice word for murder when a healthy fetus is aborted from a healthy mother who has voluntarily had sex with a father of the aborted child.

"Another thought just came to me," Sue continued. "We'll have to notify Social Services if the doctor confirms your condition. They may feel we've not been responsible foster parents."

"This wasn't your fault," Gail protested.

Sue shook her head. "I should have talked to you more about the problems young girls often face."

The phone rang just then in Sue and Mack's room across the hall. Sue started for the door. "I'll have to get that. Ginger and her father went to the game at school tonight."

Gail had finished her tea by the time Sue returned.

"It was Mrs. Miller. She's coming right over."

"Is Steve coming with her?" Gail asked, drawing in a ragged breath.

Sue shook her head. "Steve has . . . he went to the game."

Gail closed her eyes. How could he? Didn't he care at all?

When the doorbell rang half an hour later Gail was down stairs with Sue in the living room. She had never met Mrs. Miller and was not looking forward to it. Sue went to the door while Gail tried to appear as small and inconspicuous as possible at one end of the long beige sofa, smoothing her skirt over her knees.

"This is Joanna Miller, Gail," Sue said, introducing the tall blond woman who resembled her son. "And this is Gail. Gail Richards. She says you two have never met."

The woman nodded in Gail's general direction. "I would certainly have asked to meet her if I had known she and Steven had been seeing so much of each other."

Sue took Joanna's full-length leather coat, and the woman sat down across from Gail. She wore high-heeled leather boots and an off-white sweater and matching skirt. "Just how long have you and Steven known one another?" she asked. "I didn't think to ask him."

"About seven months," Gail responded.

"Gail has been with us since March," Sue explained as she sat beside the girl, reaching out to touch Gail's hand. "I believe she and Steve met shortly after she came to live here."

"Are your parents aware of your condition?" asked Joanna.

Gail shook her head.

"We're responsible for Gail at the moment," Sue noted. "I'm sure she'll tell her mother soon."

Gail was not at all sure about that, but she offered no comment. "Did Steve tell you about our talk this afternoon?" she asked. "About everything we discussed?"

Joanna drew herself up, reminding Gail of a peacock about to fan it's tail feathers. "He told me you thought he should marry you. He said he explained it was out of the question."

"Then he hasn't changed his mind." It was not a question, but a note of resignation. Gail picked at a thread on the sofa arm. "I thought, maybe, when you found you were going to have a grandchild. . . . I mean, the baby is a part of Steve and you." Her voice trailed off.

"It would be wrong for you and Steven to marry at this time. He told me you are aware of his future plans."

"He's mentioned it," Gail replied dully. "Many times."

"It appears to me, and to Steven, the only answer in this case is for a clinical abortion. And right away." Joanna turned then to Sue. "I realize you are somewhat religious, Sue. You're probably opposed to abortion. But, according to Steven, Gail does not lean in that direction. And this is, after all, her decision."

"That's right," Sue noted. "It is Gail's decision. However, a person does not necessarily have to be *religious*, as you pointed out, to disagree with abortion. Neither of us should be trying to force our beliefs on Gail."

Joanna turned without acknowledging Sue's comments as she pulled some booklets from her bag. "I brought these for you to read," the blond woman said reaching across to hand the booklets to Gail. "Dr. Miller is out of town for the weekend. He doesn't know about this—this catastrophe yet. I stopped by his office to pick these up for you. The doctor gives them to patients inquiring about abortion."

Gail took the booklets and was about to thank her. Then she stopped. It didn't seem right, somehow, to thank a woman who was asking you to destroy her grandchild. Gail glanced at the titles.

"I know this must have been a shock to you, to everyone," she spoke at last. "Especially to Steve. I've been thinking about it for weeks. At first I thought I was wrong and it would just go away—the problem I mean—if I didn't think about it. Now I'm beginning to picture the baby in my mind. This is Steve's and my child. It's your grandchild. Have you taken time to think about it like that?"

It seemed to Gail she was sitting back listening to her own voice. It was not normal for her to speak up like this. Normally she would have remained quiet, hiding her feelings. But things were different now. A life was growing inside her, someone who needed protection.

Joanna stood up. "At this moment we're talking about a fetus, not a baby. It's no more human at this point than the egg you may have eaten for breakfast is a chicken."

"Without a word, Sue went to retrieve the woman's coat.

"Read through those booklets over the weekend," Joanna said, looking down at Gail as she pulled on her coat, adjusting the collar. "We'll be in touch with you later. If you decide on an abortion I'll make the arrangements." She started to turn toward the door, stopping to look back at the girl who still sat on the sofa. "By the way, Steven said to tell you he will be busy all weekend. I understand you asked him to call." With that Joanna Miller walked out into the brisk October evening.

Sue closed the door, glancing at Gail. "I hope you didn't expect more from her. She appears so sure of herself. Personally I think she's frightened. Steve is her only son. She's had such high hopes for him. He's

Joanna's only chance for another doctor in the family. It's been an obsession with her since he was a little boy."

"I think I'll go up to my room," Gail said in a dazed voice. She had no more talk left in her. Even her well of tears had run dry. She longed now only for the peace of sleep.

3

Someone to Love

Gail went with Sue to the doctor the next morning. As Gail had expected, he verified her pregnancy. Sue told Mack when they got home but he said nothing to Gail about it, for which she was grateful. They had decided, Sue related, not to tell Ginger just yet. "I'm afraid our daughter has not been in the best of moods lately," Sue confided wistfully, adding, "I wish I knew why."

True to Joanna's word, Steve did not get in touch with Gail over the weekend, although she kept hoping he would. At first she felt it was probably his mother's idea, saying Steve would be busy. She hoped he might call once he got away from the house. But he did not.

Gail spent most of Saturday afternoon in her room. She longed to go out for a walk, but was afraid of missing Steve in case he called. Although she begged to skip church Sunday morning, Mack and Sue insisted she go with them. While they were able to make her go, she decided no one could make her listen!

She felt uncomfortable on Sunday morning following the Grants into church. She glanced down at her stomach. Could people see she was pregnant? Gail looked around. No one seemed to be staring at her.

Ginger, who had come earlier, was seated near the front with the other teens in the youth group. She sat at the far end of a pew with a long space between herself and the others. It was then Gail realized Ginger was not close friends with any of them.

Through the singing and prayers Gail's mind was focused on seeing Steve. What would he say to her when they finally saw each other again? By the time Pastor Wilkes began his sermon she was completely lost in fantasy. Steve was running down the school hall encircling her in his arms—in front of everyone—whispering his love for her and their child, promising they would be together forever. All the other kids would be shocked at Steve's admission of love. She and Steve would marry and move into a house where she would never again feel unwanted. It would be her house, a real home where their baby would always be sure its parents loved it and each other. . . .

"And so," Pastor Wilkes' words sliced into her daydream, "never forget that your problems, those things weighing you down right now, are not insurmountable. While we all have trials, with the Lord on our side, they are bearable. God is able to lift you from the depths of despair to heights of joy, unattainable in even your wildest fantasies."

Gail blinked. Had he guessed she had been daydreaming?

She listened then as the round-faced minister continued, a curl of white falling over his forehead. "And for those of you who have not yet allowed the Lord Jesus Christ into your life, let me just say this. . . ." He leaned forward, his arms on the pulpit as he looked down on them with a warmth that penetrated even Gail's cold fears. Lowering his voice, as though about to reveal a hidden secret, he added, "I have good news. Our God, whom we worship, is waiting for you with a love and acceptance you'll never find anywhere else. Let go of your doubts. Turn your life and hurts over to him. While the problems may not all fly away, he will be with you."

Then, in an almost inaudible voice, he concluded, "I'll tell you a secret most people in this world overlook. God *does* care about us—about you and about me."

Later, as Gail and the Grants shook Pastor Wilkes' hand at the door, she again felt the warmth of his smile. She mumbled something in reply to his cheery greeting, feeling her face grow warm.

His words echoed in her mind all afternoon until she drove them away by going to her room to read the abortion booklets Mrs. Miller had left Friday night. From them Gail learned more about abortion than she wanted to know. The booklets were factual, explaining life scientifically, and the abortion of life as routine as a tonsillectomy.

The next morning Lorna, Gail's only girl friend, waited on the corner to walk to school with her. Lorna always waited there, two houses down the block. Ginger usually left the house earlier than Gail. Gail figured it was so they would not have to walk together, which was all right with her.

"Hi," Lorna called as Gail approached. "Do you feel better? I wasn't sure you'd be going to school today."

Gail stopped when she reached the sandy-haired girl. Lorna was tall, rather large-boned, and somewhat clumsy. She had nice features, but her haphazard attire and stringy hair detracted from her better qualities.

Lorna and Gail had begun their friendship on the first

day Gail registered at Hillwood High. However, the bond between the two had done nothing for either of them. It had certainly not rooted Lorna out of her unwanted isolation, while their relationship had completely shot down Gail's attempt to project the new image she longed for. Instead the two girls clung to their friendship, supporting one another in a school culture neither fit into. Few of their peers even acknowledged their existence.

"What made you think I was sick?" Gail asked. With Lorna, at least, she could be herself.

"You told me you couldn't walk home with me Friday. You didn't look like you felt good, and since you didn't call over the weekend, I just figured you were sick and went home early."

Gail shook her head. "I had to talk to Steve."

"Really? What about?" Lorna's eyes brightened. She loved hearing about Gail's dates with Steve. She was always filled with questions, although Gail never told her much.

"If you're so interested in boys why don't you find a guy for yourself instead of trying to relive my dates with Steve?" Gail shot back at her.

Lorna blinked. Gail might as well have slapped her. "What's the matter with you?" she asked.

Gail sighed as she turned, starting toward school. She walked in silence beside Lorna. At last Gail glanced at her. "Oh, come on. I'm sorry. It's just that I've got a lot on my mind."

"Does Steve want you to.... You know." Lorna seemed excited about the possibilities.

"I may as well tell you," Gail said. "I'm three months pregnant."

Lorna's expression froze, then blossomed into joy. "Terrific! Oh, wow! I wish I was pregnant."

"That's a dumb thing to wish for," Gail muttered.

But Lorna's blue eyes were shining. "No it's not. Just think, now you'll have someone to love you. Someone your very own."

Gail was unnerved by her friend's reaction. She certainly had a weird way of looking at things. Or did she? Gail had hardly expected anyone to envy her. "I don't understand you at all. Here I'm feeling just awful and you act like I should be doing handstands." She flipped her dark hair back with a toss of her head.

Lorna stopped, pulling Gail off to the side as they were about to cross the street to the school campus. "Before you came here there was this girl I knew. Her name is Jill. We're sort of friends. Anyway, she got pregnant, too. She quit school and got a job. She and her baby have a neat apartment now and she's finally out of this school rat race."

"Who takes care of her baby while she works?" Gail questioned.

"Her mother, I guess."

"Well, that's where she and I are different. I wouldn't have anyone to take of a baby."

"What about Mrs. Grant?"

Gail shook her head. "She's working, remember? And I sure wouldn't want my own mother taking care of a baby, even if she didn't have to work and agreed to do it."

"What are you going to do then?" Lorna persisted.

"I don't know. I keep hoping Steve will decide we should get married. His family could afford to help. He could even go on to school."

"I wouldn't count on that," Lorna remarked. "I've heard plenty about Dr. Miller's wife."

"Come on," Gail urged, glancing at her watch. "We're going to be late. I've got enough problems right now without that."

Gail watched for Steve all day. She even spent part of

her lunch break in the hall near his locker. But he never showed up.

Lorna begged off walking home with her after school using the excuse that she suddenly realized she had some shopping to do downtown. Gail wondered if Lorna was turning their friendship off after thinking it over.

Gail and Ginger were helping Sue in the kitchen that evening after dinner when the doorbell rang. Mack opened the door to find Lorna standing there. He invited her in to wait until Gail finished helping with the cleanup chores. In the kitchen Ginger nudged Gail and whispered, "She's never come to the house before. What does she want, anyway?"

Gail shrugged.

Lorna sat toying uneasily with a small department store bag as she waited until the dishes were put away. Then she and Gail went upstairs to Gail's room.

"I brought you something," Lorna said, handing her the paper bag.

Gail took it, pulling out a flat oblong box. She turned it over. Inside the clear plastic front panel was a pale green baby sleeper.

"It's a newborn size," Lorna remarked with a wide grin. "I thought maybe you'd want to bring the baby home from the hospital in it. I got green since we don't know if it's a boy or a girl."

Her legs weak, Gail plunked down on the bed, pushing the box from her. "Oh, Lorna. . . . What did you do this for? And why bring it here? Ginger doesn't even know about the baby yet."

"Here." Lorna sat beside Gail. Carefully she took the tiny green knit garment from the box, holding it out to her friend. "Feel how soft it is. And see how small. It's hard to imagine a person could ever be that small."

Slowly Gail reached out, taking the sleeper from Lorna.

It *was* soft. She held it to her cheek and then cradled the tiny garment in her arms as if it already held her baby. She visualized the child. It would open its eyes and look up at her—its mother—and smile. It would love her as no other person had ever loved her before. It would be a boy and look just like Steve. When Steve saw it he would love her and their baby so much. . . .

At last she turned to Lorna. "The baby has never seemed so real before. You know?"

Lorna nodded. "I know," she whispered.

Gail's gaze shifted to her nightstand where the booklets Mrs. Miller had brought over were concealed. They were so technical. So cold. A baby was warm and feeling. Even now it was developing secure and safe within her. Sue had shown her a book with pictures of a fetus at each month of its development. Gail pressed her fingers to her stomach. According to Sue's book her baby's sex and much of its personality were already formed.

"Thank you, Lorna. I think you may have helped me make a decision. I can't kill my own baby. It may be just a mass of cells to Steve and his mother, but to me it's a human being. . . . Right now."

Lorna threw her arms around Gail. "Isn't it just wonderful!"

"Yeah. I guess it is. In a way." Gail smiled weakly.

Later, after Lorna had left. Gail went downstairs. She was alone in the living room reading a book. Ginger and Mack watched television in the family room. Gail sat down across from Sue. "I'd like to talk."

Sue closed her book. "All right," she responded with a smile. "How goes it tonight?"

Gail shrugged. "I'm not sure." She lowered her voice, glancing toward the room where the television emitted noise enough to cover their voices. "When we talked before, about what I should do. . . . Well, you know."

"Yes." Sue nodded.

"Mrs. Miller and Steve want me to have an abortion, while you feel it's best to have the baby, then put it out for adoption."

"Yes," Sue replied. "But you have to make up your own mind. You're the one who has to live with the decision. And yet I can't deny I'd rather see you continue the pregnancy and then release the child."

Gail swallowed. "There's still another way. What if I kept my baby? Steve says he doesn't want to get married. But maybe he would after he saw it. Lots of girls keep their babies now."

"I know," Sue responded. "But they usually have families able to stand by and help. Or else the girl is older—better able to cope with a baby. God meant children to be brought into a home complete with a father and mother—although I realize it doesn't always work out that way.

"Some girls try raising their babies alone only to find they're not able to manage either financially or emotionally," Sue added. "They and their children many times end up with enormous problems."

Gail glanced away. "I could never count on my own family. But," she hesitated, "I thought maybe you and Mack might let me stay on here with the baby for a while. Just until I got a job."

"Oh, honey." Sue was shaking her head. "You're scarcely more than a child yourself. You couldn't possibly support yourself and a baby."

"I could if you'd let us stay here until I was earning enough to find a place of our own. I'll get a job just as soon as the baby is born. It shouldn't take more than a few. . . ."

"Gail, it's not that easy finding work at your age," Sue

interrupted, "especially one paying enough to provide day care. It could take months, even years, before you'd earn enough to become self-supporting. If I weren't working I might be able to take care of the baby for a while. But my job is important. Some of those people in the convalescent center have no one else. They depend on me. Besides, if Mack and I helped you keep your baby we'd be aiding you in something we feel is wrong for both you and the child."

Fright wrapped tight around Gail again. Her baby was a very real part of her now. How could she destroy it—or give it away? "Sue, please help me keep my baby."

"Keep your what?" It was Ginger. The freckled girl stood in the doorway looking at Gail with a quizzical expression. "You're not really going to have a baby, are you?"

Sue motioned for her daughter to sit beside her. "Yes, Ginger. Gail told me about it last Friday. She's trying to decide what to do."

Ginger slumped to the arm of the chair where her mother sat. "Steve's?"

Sue nodded, then told Ginger about Mrs. Miller's visit and of Steve and his mother's abortion solution. "Gail's confused," Sue went on. "She was just asking if we'd let her and her baby stay here until she can support them both."

"And you told her. . .?" Ginger questioned. "I'd like to go on record as being against the whole thing."

"I need to talk to your father, of course, but I really don't see how Gail could raise a child alone at her age."

Ginger stared at Gail, her tone becoming thoughtful. "It must be tough. I don't think I could have an abortion, though. I suppose I'd put it up for adoption if it were me. I'd just make sure it had a good home first."

Gail sensed a softening in Ginger. She hadn't expected

that. "I don't know what to do. Sue, at least talk to Mack about it."

The woman nodded. "I will, honey, only...."

Ginger jumped to her feet, her face blazing with anger. "Mom! She's using you again. That's all she's been doing since she first came here. Can't you see that?"

"Ginger!" Sue was staring at her daughter.

But the girl had turned on Gail. "Before you came we were a close family. But you've split us right down the center, always buttering up to Mom, keeping her all tied up in your problems. How do you think that makes me and my dad feel?"

Not knowing how to respond, Gail simply got up and went back to her room.

A short time later Mack knocked on her door. "We just held a family powwow," he said when she opened to him. He stood there, arms hanging awkwardly at his sides. Mack's straight, nearly white lashes shadowed the blue-green of his eyes. "Sue and I feel it would be wrong for you to try to keep the baby."

Gail stepped back into the room. She didn't want to hear this.

Mack shoved his hands into his pockets. He appeared uncomfortable, as though he had just lost the toss of a coin. "It may seem like we don't care, Gail. But we do. The best decisions aren't always the easiest."

"Isn't Ginger the real reason you won't help me keep my baby?"

"No," Mack was shaking his head, "although I have to admit she's dead set against it. And maybe for all the wrong reasons." He came into the room, leaning against the wall by the door. "You have no idea how tough it is raising children, Gail. Right now, as much as we love Ginger, we're having problems with her.

"A baby is even more difficult. It's a 24-hour-a-day,

seven-day-a-week job. Even with a husband and a steady income, it's difficult for some mothers to cope."

He stared at the floor as silence filled the spaces of the room. Finally he spoke again. "Gail, just stop and think. Even if you could support yourself and the baby, what kind of life would the two of you have? You might very well end up resenting your own child. It could grow to resent you. Day care doesn't come cheap. You'd have very little money left. No, Gail, I agree with Sue on this. Adoption is the only way out for you and your baby."

Mack walked over to where Gail stood beside the desk, quiet tears streaking her face. He reached out, placing a hesitant hand on her shoulder. "It's your choice, of course. I just pray God gives you the strength to make the right one." With that he turned and left the room, closing the door softly behind him.

Gail crossed the room to her dresser taking the green sleeper from the drawer where she had hidden it. She was holding it against her when another knock sounded at the door. With no attempt to hide the tiny garment, she called out with resignation, "Come on in."

4

Future Promises

It was Ginger this time. She came in and closed the door, standing there watching as Gail caressed the baby sleeper. "Did you buy that?"

Gail shook her head, her dark hair catching light from the small bedside lamp. "Lorna brought it over. She said it was for when I bring my baby home from the hospital."

"Oh. . . ." Ginger shifted her weight from one foot and back again, her hands in front of her, one hand gripping the wrist of the other. She glanced away. "I . . . I'm sorry about the things I said downstairs. I had never said those words out loud before, about you and Mom being so close."

Turning, Gail looked at the strangely subdued girl. The dim lamplight darkened Ginger's greenish-gold eyes. "You're her daughter. That's something I'll never be."

"Yeah, I know. You and I hit a snag right from the start. Guess it's been partly my fault, although you haven't been so easy to get along with either."

Gail sighed. "We're different."

"You're sure right about that," Ginger replied with an exaggerated nod that sent her auburn hair bouncing. "I just wanted you to know I was sorry for what I said. Maybe if I'd been more of a friend to you, you wouldn't have gotten into this mess."

"What do you mean by that?" Gail demanded.

"I knew Steve was getting kind of wild. I should have warned you. He thinks he's so macho, especially with the girls. Any girl. He didn't used to be like that."

Gail's anger heated. "Oh? You think if you'd warned me about Steve, you could have had him all to yourself?"

"Hey, I don't want him. Not in the way you mean. I wouldn't share a boy the way you've had to with Steve."

Her brown eyes suddenly ablaze with hostility, Gail stepped closer to her foster sister. "Steve's not like that! You're talking about the father of my baby."

"Gail, you only see him once in a while on weekends. I see him with other girls all the time at games and at school activities. Places where you never go and where he doesn't take you."

"It's not that way with Steve and me," Gail exploded. "He *does* care about me. This baby *proves* it!"

"Your getting pregnant doesn't prove a thing, other than what a pushover you really are." Ginger tilted her head, extending her hands palms out as her shoulders rose in a shrug. "I told Mom and Dad about Steve just now and they thought I should tell you." She turned, reaching for the door knob. "Steve's not going to marry you, Gail. Whatever you do, it will have to be without him."

Clutching the infant sleeper to her, Gail pointed to the door. "This is still my room. Get out! I don't want to hear any more. You're jealous, that's all. And it's more than just over your mother and me being close."

Ginger backed out of the room. "I came to try to apologize. But if you don't want to listen, then that's okay with me!"

Gail went to bed still angry. Everyone was full of advice. Yet no one was willing to do anything to help her keep her baby. Ginger's, "I should have warned you about Steve," was the one brick too many on top of the Grants' turndown.

Breakfast was a silent ordeal the next morning. The walk to school only added fuel to Gail's anger as Lorna went on and on about Jill, her friend who had kept her baby, and how wonderful things were for them.

The school day passed somehow with Gail shuffling from class to class, hearing little and caring about nothing. School was supposed to prepare them for life. But all she could think of was the life already growing inside her. What did math and history have to do with this stage of her existence?

She caught a glimpse of Steve during lunch. He nodded in her general direction, but that was all. They seldom saw one another at school. She tried not to wonder about it. She used to think it was due to their schedules being so different, with him two years ahead. Could Ginger have been telling the truth? Maybe she wasn't as special to Steve as he was to her.

When she reached home that afternoon she found a note from Sue telling her to return a call from Mrs. Miller. Gail had never called Steve at home although she knew his phone number by heart. The number on the note, however, was not the Millers' number.

Gail made the call, waited, then spoke briefly to Mrs. Miller. She met Sue a little later when Sue arrived home from work. "The Millers have asked me to dinner tomorrow night," Gail told her, a wilted smile stretching her full lips thin. "Steve's picking me up tomorrow evening. His mother sounded nice this time. Do you think they've changed their minds about Steve and me getting married?"

"Anything's possible I suppose. Just don't let your hopes get too high," Sue cautioned.

Lorna was excited when Gail called later to tell her the news. "Maybe Steve wants to marry you. Wow, just think, you could be the wife of a doctor someday."

There was a lightness to Gail's walk when she met Lorna the following morning. But by afternoon she was growing apprehensive. She longed to show the Millers she could be the kind of wife Steve should have. But what if she did something really dumb like spill food in her lap? She wondered, too, what Dr. Miller would be like.

Dinner was scheduled for seven, giving Gail nearly three hours to get ready after school. By the time Steve picked her up she had changed clothes four times.

Steve was quiet on the drive back to his house. It was the first time Gail had seen him to talk to since Friday night when she told him about their baby. She didn't know what to say to him now. Light conversation didn't seem to fit when they faced such enormous decisions. And yet she could not bring herself to mention the pregnancy right then.

The Miller home was set well back off the street surrounded by evergreen trees. It appeared to be fairly new and much larger than the Grants' house. Gail wondered if she might someday have such a house as she followed Steve into the richly furnished living room.

Joanna Miller swooped into the room dressed in a long colorful peasant style dress. Her appearance took Gail completely off guard. The leather coat and boots the woman had worn the first time they met had given her an illusion of authority. This outfit made her seem much more feminine and appealing.

"Gail," she gushed, a smile brightening her carefully made up face. "I am so glad you were able to come tonight. How are you, dear?"

"Fine," Gail answered mechanically.

"I'm sorry the doctor, Steve's father, could not be here tonight. He had a meeting to attend."

Gail was both relieved and disappointed with Dr. Miller's absence. Had she been invited on the night he was away because he didn't want to meet her?

Dinner was simple. Joanna had prepared a casserole and salad followed by an enticing bakery confection. Steve remained quiet and withdrawn during the meal. The conversation flow was kept up by Joanna.

"You're certainly looking pretty tonight," the woman fawned.

Gail was glad she had finally decided on the rust print dress, one Steve had once said he liked. "Thank you," she responded, watching as Joanna poured them all another cup of tea. "You have a beautiful home. The houses are all so large along this street."

"We call it professional row," the woman said with a smile. "You know—doctors, lawyers, merchants, chiefs, and all that. I'm hoping Steve will someday have a home nearby. He should have an easier time getting started than most young doctors after his medical training, since his father will be taking him into his practice."

"Steve has talked a lot about his father," Gail noted, glancing at the boy seated across the table from her. "I can't help but wonder how Dr. Miller feels about what has happened."

Mother and son looked at one another. "He's not a judgmental man," Joanna replied at last. She rose from the table. "Would you like to see the rest of the house? We had it built to our own specificiations."

Gail started to follow the woman, then stopped, looking back at Steve who had remained at the table.

"Go on. I've seen it before," he said with a grin.

Only in magazines had Gail seen such a house. She was afraid to touch anything. When they returned to the dining room Steve was nowhere in sight.

"Let's go into the living room," Joanna suggested.

Gail followed, wondering where Steve had disappeared to. As she seated herself in a thickly upholstered chair, she had a vague sensation of being led onto a stage where she was expected to act out a part. The house was the stage. The other actors all seemed to know their parts. A caution light began blinking in her brain, alerting her to go slow before voicing her lines, to make sure they fit the plot.

She had chosen a chair in the dimly lit room by a huge picture window framed with yards of frilly cream-colored curtains held back by golden-tasseled cords. Although it was dark outside, the streetlight filtered in through the trees from the street, turning the manicured yard and curving driveway into a mystical land. "I can't imagine living in such a beautiful house," Gail ventured as Joanna draped herself in a chair.

"I don't know, Gail. You might very well have something as nice in a few years. Maybe even nicer."

"I'd be satisfied with a house like the Grants'. It's nice, too, although not nearly so large and grand as this."

"I understand you've had a less than happy childhood. Steve says your mother is alcoholic."

Gail shifted uneasily. She hadn't told Steve about herself so he could tell everyone else. "My mother has had her problems," Gail finally admitted.

"You know," Joanna noted, changing the subject, "you and Steve might very well pick up your friendship again later, after he's finished medical training. You might even become a part of this family someday." She was looking directly into Gail's dark questioning eyes.

"What do you mean?" Gail finally asked, holding her voice to a measured monotone.

"Only that a person never knows what the future holds."

"Mrs. Miller, why did you ask me here tonight?"

Joanna sighed, leaning forward intently. "I wanted you to see what your future could hold someday if you don't allow this pregnancy to ruin things for Steve now. I realize moral values have changed. But something like this—known around the community—could jeopardize Steve's future as a physician in this town. People tend to remember."

Gail steeled herself as Joanna continued.

"What I wanted to tell you is that should things work out later between you and Steve, after you've both gone your separate ways for a time and have matured, you might very well have a home such as this. The decision, however, is yours. If you have an abortion now, without anyone else finding out, you will have taken a first step in that direction."

A chill coursed over Gail, before heating to anger. Anger again. Was it becoming a part of her life? Never before had she allowed her feelings—especially anger—to pierce the shell she usually found refuge behind. "And if I take this step, you're saying Steve and I might get married someday? What kind of future would we have knowing we had destroyed our child?"

Joanna's shallow-blue eyes glazed slightly. "Didn't you even look at those booklets I gave you the other night?"

"Yes. I read them."

"Then you must see abortion is merely a medical procedure? Why do you insist on playing God by breathing life into something that's not alive, something that's just a mass of tissue?"

Gail stood up shakily. "We don't see things the same way. To me my baby *is* alive. Right this minute." She placed a protective hand over her stomach. "I'd like to go home now."

Joanna stared at the girl as she slowly stood up. Without another word the woman hurried through a door, her long flowing dress sweeping out behind her. Gail waited, standing in the center of the elaborate but cold room. She didn't want to stay one second longer.

At last Steve and his mother came into the room together. Joanna carried Gail's coat. "From what you've said, Gail, I'm left with the impression you intend to continue this pregnancy. Is that correct?" Joanna asked, her tone brittle.

Gail's hands shook as she pulled her coat on without either of them offering assistance. "I don't know for sure." She was not about to tell them she had been thinking about keeping the baby. Steve followed as she walked to the door. "Thank you for dinner," she managed to whisper as she passed Joanna.

Gail sat beside Steve in stiff silence as he backed his car around, heading out the long curved driveway. "What'd you do, leave so your mother could badger me into getting an abortion?" she demanded.

Steve said nothing as he turned the car onto the street. After a couple of blocks he glanced at her, reaching for her hand. "Gail, I don't know exactly what Mom said to you. I know she's pretty strong when it comes to things she wants and doesn't want. She told me she didn't think you understood her intentions."

"Did you know why she asked me over tonight? Did you know she planned to tell me you and I might get married someday if I got an abortion?"

Steve squeezed her hand. "I doubt she said it just like that."

"You didn't hear her. I did."

He let go of her hand and turned the car onto a side street. "Let's drive someplace and talk. Okay?"

At last, Gail thought. It was about time the two of them talked without others interfering.

Steve switched on the radio and reached for her hand again. The low rhythmic beat of the music numbed Gail's ragged nerves. When they came to the spot they had driven to so many times before, Steve stopped the car and switched the lights and motor off. He turned to face her. It was dark and moonless. She could barely make out the outline of his face from the reflected light of the radio.

"I'm sorry," Steve began, "if Mom badgered you. You're going through enough right now without that."

"How do you feel about the baby now that you've had time to think about it?" Gail asked. "Steve, have you ever loved me?"

He pulled her close. "Hey, sure I've loved you. There are all kinds of love, though. If you're talking about the kind where two people commit the rest of their lives to each other. . . . Well, I don't know that either of us is ready for that."

"What about our baby?"

His arm tightened as he pressed his angular cheek against her silky hair. "We've made a mistake. A child shouldn't be made to suffer because of what we've done."

Gail's eyes were growing accustomed to the darkness. She pulled back to look into his face. There was a troubled scowl there. "I can't kill our baby. I don't know what I'm going to do, but I know I could never end its life with an abortion. How would you feel if I quit school, got a job, and kept the baby myself?"

He did not seem surprised. "It wouldn't be easy."

"I want our baby, Steve," she whispered.

He bent to kiss her forehead, caressing her upturned

face. The music was pulsing through her. Steve's lips sought hers. "Gail, when we're together like this I.... I can't think of anything but us."

She allowed her body to melt against his. Then she stiffened, pushing away hard. "Don't! Haven't we done enough harm?"

His arms relaxed, but he continued to hold her. "Look, no more damage can be done now."

"It's wrong, Steve," Gail declared. "It's been wrong all along."

"No. It's normal."

"Not for us," she asserted. "Not now. Not just because a lot of other kids are doing it. You and I are responsible for a baby, Steve. Our baby. Yours and mine. Sex isn't just a toy. It's more than that. Can't you see? Haven't we learned anything from this?"

Suddenly he released her. His body slumped forward, his hands gripping the steering wheel, his shoulders heaving with sobs.

It startled Gail. She touched his arm. "Steve?"

5

Realities

Steve groaned softly as he leaned back against the seat. "I'm sorry, Gail. I'm sorry you're pregnant. I'm sorry I don't love you enough to marry you. I'm ... I'm just sorry!"

They sat there for several minutes, neither of them saying anything. At last he started the motor and drove Gail home. They rode in silence until the car stopped in front of the Grants' house. Gail finally looked across at Steve, but he was staring straight ahead, both hands on the steering wheel.

She opened the car door, then turned back before getting out. "I don't think I can go through with an abortion. I'll let you know what I decide. But no matter what, I never want to see you alone like this again. I thought I loved you. Now I'm not so sure."

Gail got out and walked to the house without a backward glance, hearing the car pull away from the curb as she opened the front door.

Every time she recalled her conversation with Steve's mother, Gail felt a need to bathe. She told Sue only that Mrs. Miller still wanted her to have an abortion. The rest, holding future possibilities of marriage and financial security out as an inducement to destroy the life she carried, were too painful to relive.

To Lorna's complete dismay Gail refused to discuss even with her what had happened at the Millers. "Just leave me alone," Gail cautioned as they walked to school the next morning. "Things didn't work out. That's all there is to it. The Millers are not going to help."

With marriage completely out of the question Lorna again took up the campaign to talk Gail into keeping the baby herself. "I called Jill," Lorna noted. "You know, the girl I told you about who had a baby last year. I asked if I could bring you by sometime."

"You didn't tell her I was pregnant, did you?" Gail demanded.

Lorna hesitated. "No. . . . I told her I had a new friend I wanted her to meet."

"How come you never mentioned Jill before?"

"I don't know." Lorna pulled at a sleeve of her too tight jacket.

"How old did you say she was? And what about her baby? I mean, how old is he?"

"Well," Lorna began thoughtfully, "Jill was a year ahead of me in school. I think she had to take a grade over in elementary school, so that would make her about seventeen. Her baby was born a year ago last August." She stopped to count back. "Guess that makes him fourteen months now."

"What kind of work does she do to support herself and her baby?" Gail asked, more interested then she cared to admit.

"I was wrong about that," Lorna admitted. "I asked

where she worked when I called, since I figured you'd be interested. She said she gets most of her money from welfare—although she does work once in awhile."

Gail glanced at the girl who scuffed along beside her, Lorna's run-down heels dragging on the sidewalk. "You mean welfare actually gives them money enough to live on? In their own apartment?"

Lorna's eyes brightened. "Sure! Now do you want to meet Jill?"

Gail nodded. "Guess I'd better. When can we go?"

"Jill said she's home most of the time. In fact, she said if we wanted we could have lunch with her tomorrow."

"Tomorrow's Friday," Gail remembered. "We'd have to cut class."

"What's so bad about that?" Lorna said laughing.

So Friday noon Lorna and Gail left school to catch a city bus downtown. Then they walked five blocks to an older part of town where apartments still occupied upper levels of old stores and shops, most of which had been closed and boarded up. In the building where Jill lived they climbed a narrow stairway sandwiched between two store fronts. The creaking stairs ended on a second floor, the worn carpet muffling their steps as they searched out Jill's room number.

"I thought you'd been here before," Gail whispered.

Lorna shook her head. "The last I saw her she was still living with her mother. I've never been to her apartment."

The picture of Jill and her baby secure and happy in their own attractive apartment had been painted with such realism Gail had figured Lorna to be a regular visitor. Now she was beginning to wonder about the other things her friend had told her.

"Here's the number," Lorna said stopping in front of a dark door. The varnish was cracked and chipped. She knocked.

The girl who opened to them was small. She wore jeans and a plaid shirt belted at the waist. Her feet were bare and her brown hair short. "Hi, Lorna. This must be Gail. Welcome to my abode." Jill stood back gesturing for them to enter. Gail thought Jill looked much younger than seventeen.

Lorna clowned through an introduction as Gail followed the two into a large room that evidently served as kitchen, bedroom, and living room. There was an old couch, several straight backed chairs of odd vintage, and a large round table dead center in the middle of it all. On the table was a small television set. A bed was shoved into a corner. Kitchen cabinets took up the opposite corner, along with a hot plate and small refrigerator. A scattering of toys littered the floor.

"They call this a studio apartment," Jill reflected with an abrupt laugh. "I call it a dump!"

Lorna glanced around. "Where's Timmy?"

"He's supposed to be sleeping." Jill pointed to the crumpled covers on the bed. The blankets moved and a dark curly head appeared, followed by two sleepy brown eyes. A chubby arm flew out from under the blanket as a small boy sat up whimpering.

Lorna went over and scooped up the still sleepy child. At first Timmy clung to the girl's neck. Then he stiffened and screamed. "Here," Lorna said, handing him to Jill. "He doesn't remember me. Besides," she made a face, "he's wet."

Jill took her son and set him on the floor. "He's always wet. The more I change him the more diapers I have to wash. I can't afford disposables. I'm busy now. He can wait until after lunch."

She went to the kitchen corner and began opening cans. "Hope you two like tomato soup and cheese sandwiches. They're Timmy's favorites. I've learned there's less hassle when he eats what he likes."

Timmy had stopped crying and was staring at their two visitors. He was a fat baby. Too fat, Gail thought. She figured Jill must not have too much of a problem getting him to eat.

Gail sat down on the lumpy couch and the baby crawled to her, pulling himself up to look solemnly into her face. She held out a hand, and he placed a fat finger on hers. She could see through a long tear in his plastic pants that his diaper was soaked.

"I'll change him if you'd like," Gail offered. "He seems to be making up to me."

Tossing Gail a diaper, Jill commented. "You might as well get some practice. When is yours due?"

"April. . . ." Gail glanced at Lorna who turned away. So—she *had* told Jill she was pregnant.

Timmy lay quiet, staring at Gail as she changed his diaper. Having never changed a baby before, she took special care in removing the wet diaper so she would know how to fold and pin the dry one. With the task completed Timmy rolled over and off the couch, crawling to his mother.

"Oh, for heaven's sake," Jill scolded. "Get up and walk, Timmy!" She shook her head. "He can walk. He's just too lazy."

"He's probably too fat," Lorna asserted. "Maybe his legs won't hold him. How come he's so big when you're small?"

Shrugging, Jill handed Timmy a cracker. She removed the small television from the center of the table, replacing it with a plate of sandwiches and bowls of soup. Jill added three cans of pop, and a small glass of milk for Timmy, then invited the girls to sit down.

"Lorna says you work sometimes," Gail noted. "What do you do?"

"Oh, I baby-sit, or clean a house now and then. Anything I can do so Timmy can go with me since I can't afford a baby-sitter. It gives me a little extra money now and then."

"I thought your mother took care of Timmy." Gail was glaring at Lorna.

"Not anymore. She says she's raised her kids and now it's my turn. I guess she's right. I just wish she'd decided she wasn't going to help when I found out I was pregnant. At first she told me we could live with her."

Lorna shifted uneasily in her chair as she ate her sandwich. "At least you don't have school to put up with anymore."

Timmy's young mother nodded. "Yeah, but school only lasts a little over six hours. After that you have time to do other things. Timmy and I hardly ever have a minute away from each other. I think it's as hard on him as it is on me. I'd give anything to be able to get a regular job, but child care would eat up half, or more, of everything I made."

Lorna grew thoughtful. "Why don't you find another girl who has a baby and the two of you change off baby-sitting. That way you could both get away once in awhile."

Ignoring Lorna's suggestion, Jill turned to Gail. "What are you going to do about your baby?"

"I don't know," Gail responded. "Would you keep Timmy if you had it all to do over again?"

Jill picked the boy up, holding him as she spooned soup into his mouth. "I get tired living like this. Even though I love Timmy, I actually don't know if I did the right thing or not."

Half rising from her chair, Lorna glared at Jill before sitting back down. "You did, Jill! You know you did."

Jill smiled and shrugged just as Timmy slapped his

round hand in her soup bowl spattering tomato droplets over the table. Shaking her head, she wiped his hand and then slipped him back to the floor. "I guess I'd keep him again." She handed him some crackers. "Here, eat these and be good."

The boy crawled off toward a ball, leaving a scattering of crumbs wherever his cracker-clutched fist touched the floor.

"Oh, Timmy...." Jill moaned as she went after him, scooping him up and giving his padded bottom a gentle swat. The child kicked, screaming and wiggling, until he faced his mother, his hands flaying at her face. Jill carried him back to the table. "He's such a pill sometimes," she said with a sigh. Timmy turned his tantrum off as she sat down, cuddling him to her. "But he's all I've got."

Lorna looked at Gail in triumph as their eyes met. "I've been trying to get that across to Gail. Even when no one else in the whole world cares about you, at least your child will."

Timmy was squirming to be free again. Jill wiped the crackers from his hands and placed him back on the floor to play. "That's not quite the way it works, Lorna. Timmy is a very independent little boy."

Scowling, Lorna pleaded, "Hey, don't go talking Gail out of keeping her baby. You wouldn't want her to kill it by having an abortion would you?"

"No. Still ... I'm not really sure I chose the right way either. I do love Timmy. But sometimes I almost...." She glanced away, watching as he played with the ball, then closed her eyes for a second before continuing. "Sometimes I almost hate him, his father, my mother ... everyone."

"Then you wouldn't keep him if you had to make the choice again," Gail countered.

"I can't really say that either," Jill shrugged. "I do know

I'd look into all the other ways open to me instead of trying to defy everyone the way I did. I was so sure of myself. Determined to have my way and keep my baby no matter what. Some girls may get by okay. But I feel trapped."

"I haven't been around many babies," admitted Gail. "Had you? Before Timmy was born, I mean?"

Jill shook her head.

Lorna jumped up, her chair scraping back across the floor. "I think you're both just awful," she stormed. "I'd give anything if Timmy were mine. Or if I was going to have a baby like you, Gail. All you two are talking about are yourselves. Timmy has feelings you know. He's a person, too."

Jill nodded. "Yes, Lorna, but what's he going to think of me when he's older? What about when he goes to school and I can't afford to buy him the things other kids have? What will he say when they talk about their dads? What then?"

"He's *your* son," Lorna declared.

"But what about me, Lorna? I've got a right to some kind of life, too." Jill turned back to Gail. "I did some pretty stupid things at first. The day I took Timmy home from the hospital to my mother's place I began telling him how great things were going to be for the two of us. I told him about the fun we'd have together.

"I even took my new swimsuit out of the closet to show him—the one I bought just before I got pregnant. Then I noticed he'd fallen asleep. I was hurt. After all I'd gone through to have and keep him and then he falls asleep like that when I'm talking to him!"

Jill smiled wistfully as she remembered. "Silly, wasn't it? I've learned plenty since then, believe me. Babies don't care what their mothers do or want. They've got their own needs, and that's all they care about."

Gail and Lorna remained quiet later as they walked to

the bus stop, each wrapped in her own thoughts. Finally Lorna commented, "Jill doesn't deserve Timmy. If she loved him the way she should he'd love her back."

"I think you've missed the point, Lorna. Jill does love Timmy. That's why she's questioning whether she did what was best for him."

"I don't care what either of you do or say," Lorna pouted. "I'd still like to have a baby all my own. And I will someday, too."

When Gail arrived back at the Grants she was surprised to find Sue already at home. She had planned to get back before the others. Sue explained she had left the convalescent center early to run a couple of errands.

Gail admitted she and Lorna had skipped school. She explained where they had gone and why. Sue scolded her as Gail sat at the dining room table while Sue folded a basket of clean laundry.

Picking up a drier-warmed towel to fold Gail commented, "Jill feels trapped. She can't get a job because there's no one to take care of Timmy. Evidently she doesn't get much money from welfare, 'cause she can't afford to do anything, other than stay home and watch Timmy and television all day."

"Maybe I was wrong," Sue said as she shook out a pillowcase with a snap. "You may have learned more at Jill's apartment this afternoon than you would have at school."

Gail forced a laugh. "Maybe. But Sue, lots of women have jobs as well as kids."

"As we've told you, day care is expensive," Sue reminded. "I don't imagine Jill could find a job that would pay enough to cover child care—especially since she didn't even finish high school.

"A married couple is able to share the responsibilities," Sue went on. "Jill never had a chance to really grow up herself. Now she and her baby are growing up together without the husband and father God intends a normal family to have."

"You're thinking about me, too, aren't you?" Gail noted.

Sue nodded. "When a baby's born it's completely helpless. At first it doesn't really matter who's around just as long as it's fed and dry. When it doesn't get what it wants, it lets everyone know—loud and shrill.

"Lorna's idea of having a baby so someone will love her is not realistic. A baby learns to love its parents, or the ones it thinks of as its parents. Some children never appreciate their mothers and fathers until after they have a family of their own."

Sue gathered up a pile of folded towels and placed them back in the basket.

"I don't want me or my baby to have to live like Jill and Timmy," Gail said at last. "I don't want to feel trapped by my own child." Her dark eyes pleaded with Sue as they filled with tears. "So where does that leave me? If I can't go through with an abortion, if Steve won't marry me, and now if I don't feel I should keep my baby—where does that leave me, Sue?"

The woman cupped a hand around the girl's flushed cheek. "Honey, you know where that leaves you. It brings you right back to adoption."

"No, Sue. I can't give my baby away. I just can't!"

6

The Order of Things

The promise of a cold wet day greeted Gail when she awoke on Saturday. A gust of wind rattled the window screen as her mind rounded up her troubles, lining them all in a neat row. She closed her eyes again. Solutions to her pregnancy were dwindling with each day that dawned.

Dinner with Steve and his mother had produced nothing. The drive home had been an awakening experience—more like waking from a nightmare! She and Steve had given into desires that were not right. As she realized more fully what their act had done, guilt clinched her tight, holding her hostage.

That night she finally faced it. Sex had been only a game with them. Had love ever been a part of their relationship? She wasn't sure. Their baby would be the one paying the price unless she made the right choice. There was no going back to right the wrong. It would forever be with them, whether they remained close to the child or never saw it after its birth.

The visit to Jill's apartment had dimmed Gail's dream of keeping her own baby. Jill's dead-end street was not what she wanted for either herself or her child. She was afraid of living alone like that—alone with a baby, bearing the everyday responsibilities of motherhood with no one to fall back on.

And then there was Sue and Mack's solution. Could she carry this baby for nine months only to give it away? Would her son or daughter grow up as she had with no one to love it?

As soon as breakfast was out of the way there was the usual Saturday morning house cleaning to be tackled. The work touched Gail with a sense of reality as she and Ginger helped Sue rid the house of another week's worth of living. The girls avoided one another as much as possible, which was not unusual. Gail could tell something new was astir within Ginger since she was not her normal mouthy self. Was the redhead feeling a touch of guilt over her jealous outburst? If so, Gail certainly had no inclination to ease Ginger's mind. After all, Ginger still had a mother and a father, while Gail had no one—no one but her baby.

After lunch Gail went back to her room to rest and be alone. She was tired. While she had not been experiencing much morning sickness, she did tire more easily.

It was early afternoon when Sue came to her room. "Want some company?"

Gail, who had been lying on the bed, sat up. "I guess...."

Sue pulled the desk chair around and sat down. "I've been thinking. Shouldn't you tell your mother about the baby? I'd want to know if I were her."

"You're not her," Gail said, crossing her legs in front of her, Indian fashion. "She wouldn't care."

"Aren't you making a judgment without giving her a chance?"

"Maybe," Gail spoke with a sigh. "I suppose I'll have to tell her. But I can't right now. I'm still too mixed up."

Gail hesitated bringing up the things she had been thinking about. And yet, she really needed to talk to someone. She took a deep breath and plunged in.

"I've been thinking about Steve and me. At first it . . . sex . . . seemed just a part of growing up. You know, doing those things the grown-ups were always talking about. The kids at school talk about sex like it's just a part of living. But now after what's happened, I can see why it was wrong for Steve and me."

She told Sue then about what had taken place Wednesday night when Steve drove her home. "All I could think of was the baby. Our baby. Sex had made it, even though we hadn't been thinking about a baby at the time. Whenever Steve and I were together it was like we were on a long slide. It was great on the way down. But here—at the bottom—it's real scary. Our baby's the one who will suffer for what we did."

"You and Steve are suffering, too," Sue put in. "You will always wonder about your child no matter what future you choose for the baby. Even if you were able to keep it, you'd wonder what your son or daughter's life would have been like if you had released it for adoption."

Gail wiped at a tear that got away. "I haven't wanted an abortion. I still don't. And yet. . . . I've been wondering if it might be better. I mean, if my baby is going to grow up miserable, maybe it would be better if it never lived at all."

"I don't believe ending life prematurely is ever a solution. What about adoption?"

"How can I give my own baby away? Like I didn't care anything about it?"

"I ache for you," Sue spoke, staring down at her hands

tightly clasped in her lap. "We should have spent more time talking about these things earlier."

They were silent for a time, each absorbed in her own thoughts. At last Sue declared, "Gail, I want you to talk with Pastor Wilkes. Maybe he can help with your decision."

Gail was shaking her head. "I couldn't talk to him. I mean, I just couldn't!"

"He's easy to talk to, honey. He's not going to judge you." Sue came to Gail, placing both hands on the girl's shoulders, looking deep into Gail's damp brown eyes. "He's far better equipped than I to counsel you on this."

"You mean he'll try to stuff the Bible down my throat!" Gail protested.

"No, I'm sure he won't force any ideas on you," Sue said.

Reluctantly Gail agreed to ride across town with Sue to the church office.

As Sue turned the car into the parking lot she noted, "I called him before we left, so he knows we're coming."

"Did you tell him about me?"

"Well, yes, so you wouldn't have to break it to him."

"I suppose that's better," Gail remarked with resignation. She followed Sue through a side door into an outer office. It was empty and silent. There was a closed door marked "Pastor" on the far wall. Sue crossed to it and knocked as Gail's stomach did a flip-flop. Why, she wondered, did she have to go through with this on top of everything else? There was nothing the man, anyone, could say or do for her now.

The door opened and Pastor Wilkes stood there smiling. "Well, come in. Come in," he greeted them. The man, apparently in his sixties, was wearing a powder blue button-front sweater over a light-colored tieless shirt. Gail steeled herself for the inevitable.

"I've been expecting you." He looked at Gail. "I'm glad you felt you could come to me. Makes me feel needed." His eyes crinkled at the corners as he leaned closer, lowering his voice. "You know, we pastors need to be needed!"

Gail smiled in spite of herself.

The thickset man pushed two chairs toward them, waiting until they were seated. Then he perched himself on a corner of the desk, one leg dangling. He reminded Gail of an elf—a very large elf with an impish face under a mass of curly white hair.

"You don't really want to be here, do you, Gail?" he observed. "This must be Sue's idea. Am I right?"

Gail glanced away, then nodded.

"Yes, it was my idea," Sue admitted. "Gail needs to talk to someone. I felt you were the logical choice." She stood up. "I think it would be best if I waited in the other office." She turned to Gail. "Tell him the things that have been bothering you. And what you've been considering. You can be as open with him as you have with me."

As Sue left the room, the pastor pulled the empty chair around and sat down. "I'm sure it's difficult talking about your pregnancy. Sue told me you're being pressured to decide by everyone, including her."

"That's right," Gail admitted. "And yet no one has been willing to help me do what I really want to do—keep my baby. I don't want to kill it. And I don't want to give it away. And yet I can't stand the thought of living like Jill, a girl I met who's on welfare and living alone with her baby in an awful room she calls an apartment." Gail shuddered.

The pastor crossed his legs and leaned back, pulling at one ear. "I appreciate your feelings. But, Gail, let's put your wants aside for a minute and think about the baby. What is it you want for him or her—whatever your baby turns out to be?"

Without hesitation Gail replied, "I want my baby to grow up knowing it's loved. I want it to be happy and not afraid. I want. . . ." She stopped, tears swelling her eyes. "I want the things for my baby I've never had. Mainly, love."

"You have never been loved? Ever?" he questioned.

She blushed. "If you mean, didn't the baby's father love me. . . ."

"No," he interrupted. "I was not being sarcastic. It's terrible a girl your age has never experienced love from those close to her. Surely the Grants care about you. They've always appeared to be loving parents. Perhaps too loving for Ginger's own good."

"But they aren't *my* parents," Gail protested. "They're Ginger's."

"And you feel left out."

"I've always been left out," she complained.

"What about God? He loves you."

Gail shook her head.

"You do believe in God, don't you, Gail?"

"I don't know. I've really never thought much about him one way or the other."

"He thinks about you."

She shrugged. "Why should he?"

Pastor Wilkes leaned forward, his expression turning serious. "Let's stretch our minds with a 'what if' game. What if you keep your baby. Let's say it's a boy. You give him all the love, security, and material gadgets anyone could ever want, and yet he doubts you care about him. He accepts everything you do for him as though it were owed him, but wants nothing to do with you as a person or as his mother. How would you feel?"

Since Gail did not answer, the pastor added, "Isn't that what you're doing when you ignore God, the one who's given you life?"

"It's not the same," Gail said. "A mother is with her

child, not off in heaven somewhere out of sight like God."

"Gail, those of us who follow Christ, who have taken the name Christian, *do* know him personally, just as we know our earthly parents. Not with physical eyes, but with spiritual senses. He made us all with an inborn need to love and to be loved. The highest form of that love is when he loves us and we love him in return. He wants only the best for us, just as you want for your child.

"While it's not always easy being a Christian," he noted with a smile, "it surely can get exciting at times. The Lord sticks with us through thick and thin. When you compare what he's given us, the rough times in life seem easier to bear."

"What has God ever given me?" Gail asked, sarcasm edging her voice. "A mother and father who hate me? And now a baby I have to either give away or kill?"

The minister appeared unruffled by her retort. "He's given you life and an opportunity for eternal love. His Son Jesus gave up his life here on earth just so you—and I—wouldn't have to pay our own debts for wrong. Even then God wasn't through giving. Jesus rose from the dead in a new body so his followers could see what theirs would someday be like."

"Even if he really did all that," she reflected, "I doubt he did it for me. For you maybe, but not for me."

She shifted uneasily in the chair. "But what has all this got to do with my baby, or the decision I have to make?"

Pastor Wilkes stood up, going around to sit at his desk, his forearms resting on its top. "Tell me where you are in your thinking, Gail."

"That's my problem," she said. "I don't know. I don't want an abortion. I want to keep my baby, but I don't want to have to go on welfare like Jill."

"The Grants are in no position to help you keep your

child. They have all the problems they can handle right now with Ginger. Have they told you what Ginger's threatened to do?"

Gail shook her head.

"She's talking of going to live with her grandmother in Arizona. Although Ginger was raised in the church, I'm afraid she's never yielded her life to the Lord."

So . . . Ginger hated her so much she was ready to leave home. Well, let her! Gail thought then of Sue and Mack and how hurt they would be. Ginger probably wasn't any more of a Christian than she was. "It's because of me, isn't it?" Gail asked at last.

"Ginger's problem started before you came."

"Problem? Ginger? What kind of problem does *she* have. Seems to me she's got just about everything anyone could want."

"You've found it difficult to get along with her, haven't you?"

Gail nodded.

"You're not the only one. She evidently has few friends due to the brash know-it-all tendency she's slipped into."

He reached for the Bible on the desk beside him. "But that's not your concern. You have enough problems of your own to work out. Let's get back to the baby." He opened the Book, ruffling through its pages. "While the Bible gives no 'thou shalt nots' on the subject of abortion, God does make it clear life is important to him. Let me read Psalm 139:13-16.

Gail caught the main drift as he read. Something about how God saw the writer while he was growing inside his mother, and planned out his life.

"However," Pastor Wilkes continued as he looked up, "God does give us written instructions concerning sex outside of marriage. I can assure you he's definitely against it. The union between a husband and a wife can be beautiful and fulfilling. But casual sex between single people can be heartbreaking. I'm sure I don't need to go into all the dangers involved, the diseases we hear so much about these days."

She sighed. "Okay. But now that I'm already pregnant, what does God expect me to do? Or does he even care?" She glanced up into the man's clear gray eyes. "You believe just like Sue, don't you, that God looks on abortion as murder?"

"Yes, Gail. In most circumstances. In yours I do."

"What if I kept my baby?"

"I'm sure that would be a better solution in the Lord's eyes—better than killing the child. But you've already seen the difficulties with that. Have you considered adoption?"

Gail felt the hopelessness flood over her again. "How can I go on feeling my baby grow inside of me, knowing I'll never see it, never touch it. I'd never know what happened to it, never know if my baby was loved or hated by the people who took it. How can a God who's supposed to love me so much expect me to do that?"

"Doing what's right is not always easy."

And so there it was laid out bare and cold again. Adoption was the only solution for her as far as Pastor Wilkes was concerned. "So, you believe—like Sue and Mack—that I should hand my baby over to strangers and then just walk away after it's born."

"Yes, Gail," he said. "That's what I believe to be best for you and your child over the long haul. It won't be easy. And yet I should think it would give you more peace of mind as time goes on than any of the other options."

"I wish I could be sure my baby would be loved. I couldn't stand thinking it might be growing up like me."

"I'll tell you what, Gail. There's a couple in our church who adopted a child three years ago. Why don't you and I pay them a visit Monday afternoon. Maybe it will help you come to a decision."

He didn't even wait for a reply, taking it for granted she would go. "Now," he said, coming around the desk again to sit in front of her, taking both her hands in his big ones, "I want to pray with you—for you and for your baby."

Somehow Gail knew when she left the church with Sue she had found another friend. The minister seemed to truly care about her, her problems, and her feelings concerning the child she carried. She was glad Sue had taken her to see him. She was even looking forward to going with him to visit the couple who had adopted a child.

Pastor Wilkes was waiting when Gail walked in the door from school on Monday afternoon. He greeted her with a smile that managed to radiate the warmth of the man. She wondered if this was what it might be like to come home to find a grandfather waiting for her.

"Do the people we're going to see know why we're coming?" she asked as she rode with the pastor to visit the Longs.

"They don't even know we *are* coming," he noted with an impish grin. "We'll take them by surprise. Jim Long asked to borrow some books. We'll take them by and wing it from there."

The Longs lived in a new subdivision. It appeared they had just seeded their lawn. Mrs. Long opened the door, and Pastor Wilkes introduced the plumpish woman to Gail as Jenny.

Three-year-old Peter played in the living room under a tent made from a table covered with an old bedspread. Jenny apologized for the mess. "He likes playing where he can be near me," the round-faced woman noted with a pleasant smile.

The sandy-haired boy was too absorbed in his play to

pay attention to their guests at first. Gail sat on an offered chair watching him. At last Peter left his bedspread "tent" for the security of his mother's side, staring at the strangers who had invaded his world. Jenny Long slipped an arm around him as she talked with the pastor who was explaining the books he had brought her husband. Gail sensed the unconscious love shared between mother and son. It was understood without words, a bonding that needed no display.

At last Peter drifted back to his tent, only to be interrupted when the back door opened. A man came into the room. Peter's eyes were shining as he ran to him. "Daddy!" he squealed, running to the tall, work-soiled man, landing in his father's arms.

Gail watched, thinking of Timmy and Jill. Would Timmy ever know the joy of a father catching and tossing him in the air as Peter's daddy was doing?

Later, as they were leaving, Gail turned to Jenny. The two men had gone outside to look at some shrubs the man planned to set out. Peter had tagged along with them.

"Your son seems like such a special little boy," Gail commented.

The woman smiled. "He is. He's adopted, you know. We found we couldn't have children of our own. At first it was awful. We wanted a family so much. Now since adopting Peter, the void in our lives has at last been filled. We couldn't love him more than if he had been born to us."

"Doesn't it take awhile to learn to love a child that's not your own?" Gail questioned.

Jenny tilted her head thoughtfully. "No, we've loved Peter from the very first day we were told there was a baby on the way for us. Too many people look on their natural born children as their personal possession. A child is a human being owned by no one.

"When we reach our teen years," Jenny went on, "like you for instance, we long for independence. I remember those feelings." She smiled. "You begin growing away from your parents. It's a natural part of maturing. It's especially hard on the parents who've always thought of their children as an extension of themselves."

Gail could see the woman's point. She certainly did not feel a part of her mother. But then, she reasoned, that could be because she wasn't her mother's blood daughter.

"Are you going to tell Peter he's adopted?" Gail asked as Jenny walked with her to the car.

The woman smiled again. "We already have. I'm sure he doesn't understand what it means yet. We'll tell him more as he grows older. We don't want it coming as a shock sometime in the future."

On the drive back to the Grants, Gail told Pastor Wilkes her suspicion—her feelings she had been adopted. "I don't want a child of mine growing up the way I've had to. The Longs make it seem natural. But then, Mr. Long didn't walk out on his family when Peter came into their home the way my father did. I've heard some adopted children wonder why they weren't wanted."

The pastor sighed. "That's true. There is no perfect solution, Gail. I'm sure there are hurts for the adopted child as it grows up. You're just going to have to choose the course of action that produces the least hurt."

Before leaving Gail at the Grants', the pastor told her he would keep in touch. "Call me if I can do anything at all to help."

That evening Gail came to at least one decision. She went to the kitchen where Sue was alone and told her, "I'm going to go see my mother. I'm going to come right out and ask if she adopted me. I've always been afraid to learn the truth. But now I have to know."

7

Lost Identity

When Gail called her mother that evening, Beverly Richards informed her daughter she was working the next day, but could make time to see her around three o'clock if it was "really important." Gail was to meet her mother at the Wild Wood Inn.

It had been weeks since they had seen one another, or even talked on the telephone. Gail felt nothing as she replaced the receiver. There had been no warmth in her mother's voice, no longing to see her, none of those things Gail wished existed between herself and her mother.

The following afternoon was bright and clear for the last of October. The wind had whipped across the sky during the night sweeping the clouds off to the south. As soon as Gail arrived home from school she changed into jeans, pulled on her heavy green sweater, and walked to the bus stop. She knew exactly where the Wild Wood Inn was located. Her mother had worked there off and on ever since Gail entered first grade.

She recalled her mother coming home from work complaining about the boss saying she needed a rest. As Gail grew older she realized her mother's spasmodic drinking bouts coincided with those needed rest periods. Each time her mother dried herself out and went back to work, either at the Wild Wood or some other such place.

Gail walked into the dimly lit red-carpeted restaurant and approached a waitress setting up a table with silver and napkins. "Is Beverly Richards around?"

The young woman pointed toward the back. "She's in the lounge."

Gail walked down a hallway and into an even darker room. It was difficult to see at first.

"No kids allowed in here." The bartender growled, dismissing Gail with a jerk of his head toward the door.

"Hey, that's my kid, Jim," a low throaty voice said from a booth toward the back. The lounge was nearly empty.

Gail's eyes finally grew accustomed to the dim interior. Her mother was just sitting there looking at her, making no move to greet the daughter she had seen nothing of for weeks.

"Okay, Bev," Jim spoke. "But there'll be no drinking by either of you while she's here. Understand?"

"I know," Beverly muttered, sliding out to carry her glass to the bar.

Gail figured her mother to be in her forties now. She was enticingly dressed that afternoon in a low-cut black jumpsuit.

Draining the last swallow, Beverly placed the glass on the bar with a flourish. "You're such an old fuddy-duddy, Jim." She turned, pointing Gail toward the back booth. "Come on. Let's find out why you're here."

Her mother was thinner than the last time, her hair longer, well below her shoulders. And it was even blacker than before. She appeared nervous, her blue eyes never still under heavily made-up lashes. Gail grew uncomfortable as she sat across the narrow table from this woman who was supposed to be her mother.

Beverly lit a cigarette, exhaling a thin stream of smoke from the corner of her mouth.

"How are you?" Gail finally asked, breaking the silence.

The woman twisted a stray bit of hair with a finger. "Great. How about you?"

"Not so good, really."

Her mother looked more closely at her. "You sick or something?"

"Not exactly. I just need to ask you. . . ."

"You need money! That's it!" Beverly declared.

"No." Gail shook her head. "I just need to talk to you."

"So talk, if that's what you came for. After all these weeks without hearing from you I didn't figure you came to inquire about my health."

"What about you? You could have called me," Gail countered.

"So we've grown apart. You're not a little girl anymore." The woman's tone softened a bit. "You're growing up."

Gail wanted to say, and you're growing old even if you do try to hide it. But she didn't. "I've been wondering about something for a long time now. I really need to find out." Gail stopped, her hands at her side gripping the edge of the bench. "Did you. . . . You and dad—did you adopt me?"

"Adopt you!" Beverly tipped her head back and laughed, the sound coming in a short burst. "No! We certainly did not adopt you."

"You can tell me if you did," Gail insisted, leaning closer. "I'd understand."

"Gail, if you had been adopted I wouldn't have to work like I do. I'd be living off the fatted calf like the second

Mrs. Don Richards." Tempering her tirade then, Beverly looked steadily at Gail, her voice shrouded in resentment. "No, you were not adopted. I felt every pain of your birth. I'll feel it until the day I die."

Gail had not expected such an outburst. "I always knew you and Dad didn't want me. I thought it was probably because I was adopted. I don't look like either of you. Aaron looks like you. Both you and Dad have been closer to him than you ever were to me."

"I wasn't the one who walked out, was I?" Beverly noted. "Don left us. And all because of you."

"Me? I was only a baby when he left. I don't even remember him living with us. How could it be my fault?"

"Because you're not his, that's why," the woman spit out, staring directly into Gail's dark eyes for the first time since she had sat down. "The reason you don't look like Don is because you most likely look like your father, whoever he may be."

The remark stunned Gail, confusing her. "Then you're saying I *was* adopted."

The black-haired woman took a long drag from her cigarette, blowing the smoke out before answering. When she did her voice was low and under control again. "No, Gail. I felt every pain of your birth. Guess I always will. You're my natural daughter all right. Actually, you're what they call illegitimate."

A chill turned to pain, twisting Gail's insides. "But if I was actually born to you how could I be illegitimate? You and Dad were married. Aaron was born four years before me. Dad didn't leave until after I was born. So how...."

She stopped. Her mother just sat there looking at her, the blue of her eyes revealing nothing. "You mean you're my mother but Dad's not my father."

"Now you got it." Beverly was slowly nodding. "That's what I mean. You're the reason Don left and married that other woman. I figured you'd catch on when you got older. I didn't think anyone would ever have to spell it out for you. Haven't I always told you you're the only one on either side of the family with brown eyes?

"It's all Don's fault, you know." The woman was beginning to ramble. "He went off to Alaska to work. I got so lonely I began working nights. Once in a while one of the guys would take me home." Her eyes were half closed.

"When I found I was pregnant with you, I took Aaron and we flew to Alaska to visit Don. I wanted him to think you were his baby. But no, you had to be born early, weighing over eight pounds. There was no way you could have been an eight-month baby. Then, when he saw those big brown eyes of yours that refused to turn blue, he accused me of everything he could think of. One night I got mad. I'd had all I could take. I came right out and told him the truth. All of it. That was when he packed a bag and left."

Gail was sure her heart had stopped beating. She felt she would suffocate. Would she die right there in that darkened lounge? She watched her mother dab at a tear that threatened her mascara. Was the tear for herself, her lost husband, or for her daughter?

When the girl was at last able to speak again, she asked, "Who is my father?"

Beverly raised one shoulder in a tired shrug. "How should I know. I was drinking pretty good about that time. They took advantage of me, you know. All of them. It wasn't my fault. Don shouldn't have left me and Aaron alone that way."

"You mean you don't even know which man was my father?" Disbelief strangled Gail's words.

Beverly nodded. "That's what I mean. And don't act so high and mighty. If it hadn't been for you I'd still be married. I'd have all those things Don's given his second wife.

Look at Aaron. At nineteen he goes off to live with his father and that woman after *I* raised him. *Me.* And nearly alone. Everyone's turned against me. Even you. I could have had you aborted, you know. But I didn't."

"Maybe you should have." Gail slid out of the booth and stood up. Her legs felt wooden. "I've got to go."

Beverly slowly eased herself to her feet. "Found out all you wanted to know?" she inquired with a hint of sarcasm.

Gail hesitated. "There's one thing more. I think you should know I'm pregnant. I was afraid to tell you. Afraid you'd get mad. But I guess you don't have that right, do you?"

The woman weaved slightly, placing a hand on the table to steady herself. Gail stood there looking at her for a long moment feeling nothing. Her mother was even more down and out than she was. Gail turned and walked out of the room. When she reached the hallway leading to the main dining room she heard her mother's low voice ordering another drink.

Illegitimate! The word echoed in Gail's head as she walked the streets, blind to traffic and people. She was illegitimate. Just like the baby she carried. Who was her father? What kind of man was he? Would he have cared about her if he had known she was his daughter? Maybe he was someone she ran into from time to time, neither of them knowing they were father and daughter.

She felt guilt, too. Her birth had caused her mother's marriage to break-up. It explained why her father—or rather the man she used to think of as her father—would have nothing to do with her. Maybe her mother wouldn't be drinking so much if Gail had not been born. But then, her mother admitted she had been drinking a lot even before she got pregnant the second time. There was Aaron, too. Her brother. Or rather her half brother.

Aaron had been deprived of his father while he was growing up because of her. It wasn't fair. Not to any of them.

Gail walked until her legs and back ached. Finally she reached a railroad crossing. An old abandoned warehouse stood nearby. She climbed to the dusty platform and sat down, her back against the side of the building. She pulled her knees up, embracing them with her arms. She was exhausted. What was she going to do?

Her mother's words kept coming back. "You're illegitimate." It would have been easier to have learned she'd been adopted. How could she ever live with this?

"I don't want to live at all," Gail spoke aloud to the darkening sky. "Why not abort myself? Right now. Why not just end it all right here? Maybe that's what my mother should have done with me when she found she was pregnant. She should have had an abortion. She should have killed me."

Gail stared at the steel railroad tracks. She visualized a train grinding along the rails, coming toward her. All she would have to do was wait, then step onto the tracks a second before the train reached her.

The vision blossomed into fascination. But the tracks were rusty and old. It had evidently been years since a train had run those rails.

Another thought planted itself. If she killed herself she would be killing her baby as well. She had not made a decision about that as yet. She stood up, brushing at her clothes. She had to have more time to think. Leaving the warehouse she started on, not knowing or caring where.

Much later, tired and cold, she found herself on the street where Steve lived. It was dark now, the blackness pierced only by streetlights and an occasional passing car. All she remembered was walking fast and far, her mind keeping pace with her stride. She had no idea how she had ended up here.

Gail stopped in front of the Miller house. A light warmed the living room window at the end of the winding driveway. She turned away, then stopped again. She was too tired to walk any further. There were no buses in this neighborhood. Maybe Steve would be home. She would ask him to drive her back to the Grant home.

Swallowing what little pride remained, she walked up the cement drive and pressed the front doorbell. As she heard it chime inside, she shivered.

A tall man in shirt-sleeves opened the door. He smiled, a sand-colored mustache bristling his upper lip, his wavy hair the same shade. "Hello? And what would you happen to be selling this evening, young lady?"

"I—I'm not selling anything. Is Steve home?"

"Oh. . . . You're a friend of Steve's? I'm sorry. He's not home right now."

"Are you Dr. Miller?"

"Yes. And you are . . . ?"

"Gail. Gail Richards." She waited for him to realize who she was, but there was no glimmer of recognition. "I'm the one they told you about."

He seemed even more puzzled.

"I live with the Grants."

"I'm sorry. I don't know what it is I'm supposed to be catching onto here." He seemed perplexed.

"I'm the one who's pregnant with Steve's baby," she blurted out.

The man's face drained of color. Stepping back he held the door wide open. "I think you had better come in."

Gail followed him into the living room where Joanna was watching television. Slowly the woman rose to her feet when she saw Gail, her face paling.

The doctor looked from the girl to his wife. "It's evident you two know one another."

"May I sit down?" Gail asked, trying to control her

shivering. "I've been walking for hours. I didn't realize where I was until I found myself on your street."

Dr. Miller motioned for Gail to sit on the sofa. He looked more closely at her, then spoke to his wife. "Joanna, bring this young woman something hot to drink. Hot chocolate, perhaps."

Joanna hesitated. "I need to talk to you, Philip."

He glanced at his wife. "We'll talk later. Now do as I asked."

Gail had not realized how cold she was until she entered the warm house. Dr. Miller left, returning with a blanket. He made her lie down, then covered her.

"They didn't tell you about me, did they?"

He shook his head. "No, but I intend to be brought up to date now. I felt something was wrong. But I had no idea it was anything like this."

Joanna told her husband what she had been keeping from him when she returned with the hot chocolate. Gail sat up, quietly drinking from the steaming cup as she listened to the woman's version of Gail's pregnancy.

The doctor turned to the girl. "You've been under the impression I knew about this?"

Gail nodded. "I figured you were angry, and that was probably why you weren't here last Wednesday night when Mrs. Miller asked me to dinner."

Joanna avoided her husband's eyes when he glanced at her again. A muscle twitched along his jawline. He sat down beside Gail, taking the empty cup from her and placing it on an end table. "You said you had been walking. Besides being tired, how do you feel?"

"All right, I guess," she responded. "I went to see my mother. I thought maybe she adopted me when I was a baby. I needed to find out, since I'm trying to decide what to do about my own baby."

Embarrassment flowed over her. Why was she running

on and on like this? It wasn't like her. She looked down at her hands lying idle in her lap. She wished she had not come to their door.

"Did your mother satisfactorily answer your question?" the doctor probed.

The girl shook her head.

"What made you think you were adopted?"

"Because. . . ." She couldn't bring herself to go into all the whys. "She didn't adopt me. She told me I'm illegitimate. Just like my baby's going to be." Tears coursed down her face. "My father—I mean the man I thought was my father—left after I was born when he found out I wasn't his. No wonder he's never wanted anything to do with me."

Sobs tore at her as her words tumbled out naked and bare. "I was born to a woman who didn't want me. She blames me for breaking up her marriage. But it wasn't my fault she got pregnant. Now I'm as bad as she is. And. . . . Oh, why am I telling you all this?"

Gail threw the blanket aside and stood to her feet. "I'm sorry. I was wrong coming here. I'm. . . ." Her legs buckled and she started to fall.

The doctor moved quickly to catch her. "Joanna, get my bag," he said as he placed Gail back on the sofa.

After checking the girl's blood pressure and pulse, he said, "You're exhausted. I'll drive you home. You should feel better by tomorrow."

Joanna came to stand behind her husband. "What do you intend to do, Philip? You must see, from what this girl has just told us, none of this is Steven's fault. Girls like her get our boys into trouble all the time, then go running to the parents for help."

"That's enough, Joanna! I want you to get on the phone and locate our son. I'll talk to him—and to you— when I get back."

Dr. Miller waited in the Grants' living room while Sue helped Gail into bed. Then he went up to her room and administered a mild sedative. "I'll see you again soon. We need to talk. I want you to know I do not condone whatever tactics my wife has been using. But right now you should get some sleep. I think it would be best if you stayed home from school tomorrow."

Gail nodded. He squeezed her hand, pulling the blanket up around her shoulders. As he left Gail could visualize what it would be like to have a father who cared. A loving mother was important to a child. She knew that. But a father's love, whether gentle, stern, or boyishly playful like Mack, could never be grafted in by all the extra mothering a woman could muster.

She placed a hand on her stomach as her eyelids grew heavy. "I've got to find you a father, Baby. One who will love you the way you deserve to be loved."

Gail slept late the next morning. Ginger and Mack were gone by the time she came downstairs. She was surprised to see Sue still there. "I called to tell them I wouldn't be able to work today," the woman explained as she fixed Gail's breakfast. She sat down then with a cup of coffee while the girl ate.

"Did Dr. Miller tell you what I found out from my mother yesterday?" Gail asked.

"Yes," Sue acknowledged. "Earlier Mack called your mother when you didn't come home. We figured something must have gone wrong. He said it sounded as though she had been drinking. We were worried and about ready to call the police."

Gail told Sue all that she had found out. "It's even worse than if I'd learned I was adopted. A lot worse."

Gail dozed on the living room couch off and on that day, staying close to Sue.. She couldn't bear to be alone. Sue encouraged her to think about her mother and the man she had thought of as her father. They discussed the problems that had pressured the Richardses into one mistake after another.

"I'm not making excuses for them," Sue noted. "It's just that it helps sometimes to try to see things from the other person's point of view. Even if you disagree."

By evening Gail was feeling better, at least physically. Ginger avoided her until they sat down to dinner. The redhead had barely opened her mouth with a wisecrack when Mack doubled his fist, striking the table hard. "I want no more of your smart undercuts, Ginger. And starting right now!"

Ginger blinked, her mouth agape.

Lorna called later, but Gail asked Sue to tell her she didn't feel like talking. Lorna's call was a surprise. The two had not been all that close since their visit to Jill's apartment and their disagreement afterward.

Pastor Wilkes phoned, too. After receiving a go-ahead from Gail, Sue related what had occurred the day before during Gail's visit with her mother. When she hung the phone up at last, Sue said, "He would like to talk to you again."

It was still early when Gail went to bed. She fell right to sleep, even though she had napped that day. It was still dark when she came wide awake. It seemed like it should be morning. But according to the clock it was not even midnight.

She lay there staring up at the shadows reflected on the ceiling from the streetlights shining up through the bare tree limbs. She had been so tired all day she had not been able to think about her baby's future. But her muddled brain had at last cleared, opening her mind to the situation before her.

Her mother's admission about not knowing who Gail's father was had sidetracked all questions of her own child's future. Before seeing her mother she had been concerned about giving her baby up for adoption. She had worried about her child learning it had been given away by its natural parents. How would he or she handle the fact that it might never know its real parents?

Now she was faced with an even greater void. Her real father's identity was lost to her forever. Could she live with that?

Gail begged off going to school the following morning. "I need more time," she told Sue. "I want to see Dr. Miller."

Sue finally agreed.

A call to the doctor's office brought a positive response, with Steve's father telling her he would make time to see her at noon.

8

The Doctor's Plea

After an early lunch Sue drove Gail to Dr. Miller's office. The waiting room was empty when they entered. Gail stepped to the receptionist's window and gave her name before sitting down. Ten long minutes followed, stretching to eternity.

Sue touched Gail's hand. "I'm praying for you."

Gail swallowed and forced a smile. "Thanks."

At last a door opened and Dr. Miller appeared. He nodded to Sue. "I'm sorry you had to wait. I was on the phone." He looked at Gail. "Would you like Mrs. Grant to come in with us?"

Gail shook her head.

He held the door open and she stepped into a hallway, following the doctor back to a small office filled with books. After visiting his home she expected something much more grand.

He gestured toward a chair in front of his desk and then sat down across from her. "I'm glad to see you've recovered from your exhaustion. We have a lot to talk over. I've been giving the situation a great deal of thought."

Gail noticed for the first time just how much Steve looked like his father. She at first thought he resembled his mother.

"I've talked to Steve," the man said, plunging right to the point. "First, I want to apologize for the sham he and his mother pulled when they asked you to dinner. I realize they gave the impression I knew about the pregnancy. I didn't.

"Steve is absolutely floored by it all. He can't seem to pull his thoughts into focus. But I'm not offering that as an excuse for what he and his mother tried to do. It was wrong." The man appeared to be as uptight about this meeting as Gail. "Steve told me he feels the baby is his."

Glancing away, Gail held herself in check. Of course the baby was his!

The doctor was continuing. "Mrs. Miller felt an abortion was the only course of action at first."

"I know," Gail responded tonelessly.

"What I need to know is what you want to do, Gail."

"I want to keep my baby. I won't end its chance to live with an abortion."

"Do you still want Steve to marry you? He told me there was some talk of that when you first told him you were pregnant. I asked how he felt, but found no expression of love on his part."

"I know. He told me."

"Marriage is difficult at best, Gail, even when there is love. Without it I'd say it is next to impossible. Personally, I see no future for the two of you as a couple."

"I'm not expecting Steve to marry me now. I thought about it at first, but not anymore. I just want to keep my baby."

He leaned back in his chair. "How would you support yourself? And the child? You still have two more years of high school."

She gathered her courage around her, unconsciously placing a protective hand on her stomach. "Would you be able to help me? With money, I mean. Just until I found a job. I could quit school right away."

He folded his hands, staring down at them. At last he raised his eyes to hers. "Gail, you have no idea the hardships you'd be facing. You're only fifteen. Your education is nowhere near complete. Where would you find a job that paid enough to support the two of you anyway.

Without waiting for a reply, he went on. "At first I agreed with my wife. Abortion seemed the only solution. I've never handled abortions here, but I do offer abortion information. Until now it has never been an issue with me, one way or the other."

"But this baby is a part of Steve," Gail interjected. "It's your grandchild."

"Yes," he agreed. "And that is just what has caused me to take another look at abortion. It's become much more personal—so much so I could never suggest that you abort this fetus. As you pointed out, the baby is my grandchild, after all. My first grandchild. I'd like to see the baby live. Watch it grow."

Hope surged through Gail for the first time in days. "Then you will help me keep my baby?"

He appeared hesitant. "An unmarried girl of your age is not well enough equipped to handle the full-time care of an infant, Gail. You're scarcely more than a child yourself."

Hope escaped again, as despair gathered itself to pounce. "So what do you expect me to do? You say I'm too young to keep my baby. Marriage is out. You don't want me to have an abortion. The only thing left is adoption and if I do that there's no way you'll ever see your grandchild."

"Gail," he leaned toward her. "I want to adopt this child. We were unable to have any more children after Steve was born. I've always wanted a larger family. I'm certain I could love this baby as though it were my own son or daughter."

Gail sat there stunned. What did he think she was? "You expect me to just hand my baby over to you?"

"I'm sure you love the child, Gail. That's why I am making this suggestion. Mrs. Miller and I, as well as Steve, can afford to give your baby more than the average family."

She stood up abruptly. "No. I won't have *my* baby raised by *your* wife. She wanted me to kill my baby. Remember? I'd never give her my baby. And Steve sure doesn't seem to care anything about the baby." Her tightening throat choked off the rest of her objections.

"You're underestimating the depths of Steve's feelings," the doctor said in defense of his son.

"What about your wife? I sure can't see her taking care of a baby."

"We've talked it over. I told her I would hire someone to help out. And, Gail," he motioned for her to sit down again, but she ignored him, "I am also prepared to help you after you've completed high school. I thought perhaps you might like to take a secretarial course."

That was the final blow. "I'm not about to sell my baby! Not to you or to anyone," she said, backing toward the door.

"I don't want to buy the child." He was on his feet now. "I want my grandchild. All I'm offering is the chance to give the baby, and you, a more promising life."

She was shaking her head as she opened the door.

"'Thanks! But no thanks." She stepped out into the hallway.

"Gail?"

The girl turned. He was leaning over the desk, both hands flat on the top. His business-like air had dissolved away. His eyes were pleading.

"Gail, please. . . . At least don't end this baby's life."

She stood there without moving for a moment. Suddenly she felt sorrow for the doctor. The man. The grandfather. Joanna's husband. "I won't. I promise."

A strained smile twitched his mustache. "Thank you."

Once in the car Gail told Sue about the doctor's proposal.

The woman appeared surprised. "I would never have guessed in my wildest imaginings they might want the baby. I can't see Joanna mothering a child again after all these years."

"Me either. I'm sure it's all Dr. Miller's idea. Actually . . . he seems nice." Gail turned thoughtful. "Guess I shouldn't have yelled at him. At least he doesn't want me to kill my baby."

The car rolled to a stop in their driveway. Sue was about to get out when Gail stopped her. "Do you think Pastor Wilkes would be too busy to see me right now? I'd like to talk to him."

Gail waited in the car while Sue ran into the house to call the pastor, returning to tell her it was all right. And so they drove back across town to the church.

"I'd like you to come in with me this time," Gail said to Sue as they walked across the parking lot.

The pastor's door was open when they entered the outer office. He came to greet them, extending a hand to Sue. Turning to Gail he encircled her with his arms, giving her a firm reassuring hug. It startled her. She was not used to such displays of affection.

"Gail," he said, his voice heavy with empathy, "Sue told me of your visit to your mother. I wish I could have spared you the hurt. I'm praying that God will give you strength."

As the three entered his office Sue told him what had occurred that afternoon at the doctor's office.

Pastor Wilkes shook his head, directing his words to Sue. "It's a shame a beautiful child such as Gail has to be plunged into adulthood in this manner."

He looked at the girl. "None of us are able to soften the hurts you've been through. How you handle them, and the decisions you make as a result of them, are what's important now.

"Don't allow yourself to wallow down there in the pain pit, Gail. Don't wrap the hurts so tight around that you're never able to work free. You've got to stand firm. I'm confident, with the Lord's help, you'll be able to step out of this despair you must be feeling. Those of us who care about you will do all we can. But remember, God is the only one able to work the hurts out for your good."

"You prayed for me the last time I was here," Gail remarked. "Would you do it again—now? I've made a decision, I think, but I so much want it to be the right one."

Pastor Wilkes came around the desk to stand behind the girl. He placed a hand on Gail's shoulder. "Lord, I thank you right now for the love Gail feels for this child she carries. I thank you, too, for Gail herself.

"I come to you, as does her foster mother—two of your followers—asking that you grant this girl the wisdom and peace she needs in making the right choice for herself and her baby. We ask, too, that you in someway make yourself known to her. Allow this child, who now carries a child, and who has known so little love, feel and sense your love and healing presence. We ask this in the name of Christ our Savior."

A warmth blanketed Gail as the pastor moved back to sit at his desk again. "Thank you," she whispered.

Sue was dabbing at her eyes.

"Now, Gail," the man was saying, "you said you had come to a decision."

The girl nodded. "As I see it I have no other choice. I'm going to carry my baby until it's born, then let it be adopted."

Sue glanced at her, the woman's eyes wide. "You're going to give the child to the Millers?"

"No, never! I want to find a couple who will really love this baby the way it deserves to be loved. I know there are places who find parents for babies like mine."

It was impossible for the pastor to hide his relief. "I'm so glad, Gail. I'm sure you will feel increasingly confident you have made the right decision."

Sue's eyes were moist with a hint of sadness. "Are you strong enough to see this through, honey?"

"I feel stronger than I've ever felt," Gail responded. "I know this is right. Since I can't become unpregnant without an abortion, I want to give my baby life. That's the least I can give him or her."

She turned back to Pastor Wilkes. "I just want to be sure the adoption people find a couple who will truly love this baby. I'd like it to be their only child. At least their first."

"We'll help you all we can," he said. "I can appreciate how difficult this is for you."

Gail nodded. "It's a relief to finally have my mind made up, though. I dread the whole thing, but I'm determined to go through with it. It hasn't been easy accepting the fact I'll never know my real father, who he is, what he does, or what he's like. But there's nothing I can do to change that. It's made me see if I can live with those facts, then my child can too.

"There *is* another reason. If I keep the baby the Millers might try to take it away from me. I want to make sure Joanna Miller never gets hold of this child—although I do feel kind of sorry for Dr. Miller." Gail flashed a quick grin. "But—I feel sorry for me, too. He'll have to work out his own hurts. Just like me."

9

Letter to the Unborn

It was a rainy Saturday morning with a hint of snow starching the cloud-laden November sky. Sue and Gail were cleaning the upstairs while Ginger tackled the downstairs vacuuming. Ginger had announced earlier that instead of taking turns, as she and Gail usually did, she would take over the heavier work. Her offer and civil tone caught Gail off guard. Mumbling a thank you Gail headed up the stairs to start on the bathroom.

Gail was at last settling into the idea of her baby, now over four months into its development, being placed with an adoptive family. It still hurt, but there was a feeling of rightness about it. For the first time in her life she was doing something totally right—noble even. She was being the kind of mother she had always dreamed of having, sacrificing willingly for her child.

She had been thinking a lot about the people who would be adopting her baby, wondering what they would be like and if they would ever tell the child he or she had parents other than themselves. Maybe her son or daughter would try to find her someday. She hoped so. Her main fear was that it might grow up thinking its real mother had not wanted it.

Her thoughts raced as she cleaned the upstairs bathroom that day. It was there, while on her hands and knees scrubbing out the tub, that an idea came to her. As soon as she finished she went to Sue and Mack's bedroom door. Sue stopped her dusting when Gail appeared in the open doorway.

"I've been thinking about giving my baby up," Gail began.

"You haven't changed your mind, have you?"

"No. But I'd like to write a letter to the baby for when it's older, when it questions who its real mother was and wonders why it was given away. Do you think the people who adopt my baby would agree to that?"

"I don't know." Sue shook her head. "I'm not sure they could be made to give their child a letter from its natural mother. But we could ask. Pastor Wilkes is looking into adoption agencies. Just what is it you want to write?"

Gail shrugged. "I'm not sure. I want my baby to know I love it, and that I gave it up so it could have a home with a mother *and* a father. It's important to know you're loved. I'd like to have known. . . ." The girl's voice ran down to nothing.

"Why don't you go ahead and write the letter. We'll take it with us and see what the people at the agency have to say," Sue suggested.

That night Gail labored over her letter, ripping up everything she wrote and starting over again and again. At last she decided to put it off until later. She needed more time to think of what to say.

The next morning at breakfast Sue told the girls a

woman from the social service office would be coming by late that afternoon. "I called and informed them of the situation," she added. "They had to be told."

"Were they surprised when they found out about me?" Gail inquired.

Sue shook her head. "They didn't say one way or the other."

"It figures," Ginger put in.

"What's that supposed to mean?" demanded Gail.

"Oh, nothing."

"Ginger," her mother spoke, her voice sharp, "I've had all the lip from you I intend to tolerate. Understand?"

Ginger pushed away from the table. "I sure do! Little Miss Sweet Gail here, has to be protected. Right?"

Handing her daughter a stack of books from the table, Sue watched Ginger with sad eyes. "Go on to school. I'll talk to you tonight. I'm already late for work, and I have to leave early to be back here this afternoon."

The woman who rang the Grants' doorbell later that day was young. She introduced herself as Miss Hendricks. Ginger busied herself in the kitchen starting dinner while the woman talked with Gail and Sue.

There were the obvious questions. What did Gail want to do about her pregnancy? Was the father able to help? Gail hated giving her Steve's name, but Sue insisted it was the thing to do. Miss Hendricks agreed, pointing out it would not be right for taxpayers to bear all the expenses when the family of the baby's father could well afford to contribute.

Before the woman left she asked Gail, "Where do you plan to wait out the delivery of your baby?"

Gail's dark eyes widened. "I—I don't know. Here, I guess. Unless...." Gail turned to Sue.

"She's more than welcome to continue living with us," Sue responded.

"I just thought she might be more comfortable somewhere else." Miss Hendricks smiled. "Gail, you know about the Salvation Army home for unwed mothers, don't you? We've sent a number of girls there. It's easier sometimes to be with other girls in the same situation.

"The greatest asset is the school. The girls continue their classes in a small modern school building with certified teachers. Since the girls are all in the childbearing stage, there are none of the whisperings or ridicule that sometimes takes place at the public schools."

It was a new thought for Gail. The idea appealed to her.

Mack arrived home from work then, entering the living room to meet Miss Hendricks. Ginger followed him in from the kitchen, sitting on the arm of his chair. When told about the home, Mack offered no advice other than noting, "It's Gail's decision."

Ginger stood up. "Well, if you want my opinion...."

"We don't!" her father said pulling her down again.

"Do I detect a problem here?" Miss Hendricks inquired, concern furrowing her brow.

"Not really," Sue said in an effort to pass it off.

Gail looked from Ginger to Miss Hendricks. "I think I'd like to go. It will probably be better for us all."

"I checked before I came today. A couple of the girls are leaving just before Thanksgiving. Would you like me to reserve a place for you, Gail?"

Another move. Another home. Once more she was being shuttled off. Only this time the choice was hers. Ginger's attitude was a little better, but still not good. Dr. Miller would have less opportunity to pressure her into turning her baby over to them if she was away from here. Yes, it would be best to go to the home. A chill creased Gail's spine as she finally looked up. Avoiding Sue and Mack's eyes, she nodded. "Yes, put my name down for Thanksgiving."

The next day Pastor Wilkes brought a list of adoption agencies. Sue and Gail took the list to Miss Hendricks who pointed out the one she felt would be best. Gail asked if Pastor Wilkes could go with them when the appointment had been set.

And so Sue, Mack, and Gail met the pastor and Miss Hendricks at the adoption agency two days later. Gail gave the man there a list of her requests, and he agreed to locate a couple who as yet had no children. The man felt there would be no problem in finding someone willing to hold a letter from Gail to her baby, giving it to the child when it was older.

On Monday, when Gail told Lorna she was going to the Salvation Army home to have her baby, the girl smiled knowingly, flipping a straggly strand of hair back from her cheek. Their friendship continued to balance on a thin edge. Gail was too tightly wrapped in her own problems, and Lorna felt left out of all the happenings. Gail had been catching Lorna in too many half truths lately to feel comfortable confiding in her anymore. She just couldn't trust her.

"Once you get to that place and see all those other girls living there with their babies, I'll bet you change your mind real fast and keep yours," Lorna declared.

"Oh, come on, Lorna. The girls don't live there with their babies!" Gail countered.

"No? I've heard lots of girls stay right there after their babies are born. That's where I'm going if I get pregnant before I'm married."

Gail tried changing the subject, but Lorna was rambling on and on. Gail was relieved when they finally reached her corner.

Two days later Miss Hendricks called to tell Gail it had been arranged for her to go to the home the Monday after Thanksgiving. It was decided Gail should drop out of school right away, since the baby was starting to show. She would resume her schooling at the home.

Pastor Wilkes came by a couple of times to see Gail, letting her know he continued to pray for her and would always be only a phone call away in case she needed him. He never pressured her about God. At first it relieved Gail. But now she was beginning to wonder why. Maybe he didn't feel she was good enough for God.

The week before Thanksgiving Steve and his father came to the house. It had been awhile since Gail had seen Steve. She hadn't seen Dr. Miller since that day in his office when he asked to adopt her baby. They declined an invitation to sit down. Steve remained near the door appearing awkward and uncomfortable.

"We were told you're going away to have the baby," the doctor spoke to Gail as she and Sue stood together by the stairway. "You're planning to put the child up for adoption?"

"Yes," Gail replied, wishing Steve would look at her.

"You won't consider allowing us to take the child?"

Gail shook her head.

"Steve *is* the father," the doctor reminded, his tone remaining gentle.

"He's not the one who seems to want the baby," Gail fired back.

Steve raised his head, glanced at her, then turned away, his hand on the knob of the door.

The doctor closed his eyes briefly. When he opened them Gail noticed a deep sadness there. "Evidently there's no more I can say. The social services agency contacted us. I will be paying for your stay. I'll also set aside a little extra for your personal needs while you're there."

Gail shook her head. "I have all I ever want from the Miller family, thank you." Her fingers touched her growing stomach bulge. She regretted her words as soon as they escaped.

Choosing to ignore her brush-off, Dr. Miller stepped closer. He reached out hesitantly, placing a hand on her arm. "Gail, I wish I could do something to make this easier for you. You may not believe that, but it is true."

Blinking her tears under control, Gail stood in the open doorway watching them walk down the steps toward the car. She was closing the door when Steve glanced back and waved. With the door shut Gail dissolved to tears in Sue's arms.

Ginger came from the family room where she and Mack had remained out of the way. "Gail . . ." the auburn-topped girl spoke. "I wish. . . . I'm sorry for everything that's happened between us. And—well, I just want to say, if you decide to stay here it's okay with me."

Shaking her head, Gail pulled away from Sue and started for the stairs. Halfway up she stopped, looking down at Ginger. "Thanks anyway. But I have to go."

On a chilly afternoon before moving to the Salvation Army home, Gail went to see Pastor Wilkes once more. After calling the pastor to ask if it would be all right, she struggled into a heavy hooded jacket and lined boots, striking off across town alone. Chilled snow-heavy clouds spit loose lazy white flakes, threatening more before long. It was good being outside, breathing in the crisp end-of-autumn air. It felt good having to walk fast to keep warm.

She reached the church and knocked at the pastor's door, telling him when he opened it she had come to thank him for his help. However, that was not the whole of it. She actually had something else on her mind.

"Do you think God can ever forgive me for what I've done?" she asked once they were seated inside.

The grandfatherly man smiled. "He's already made provision for that, Gail. He's just waiting for you to ask."

Crossing an arm over the other, the pastor leaned back. "Getting pregnant isn't the worst thing anyone's ever done, you know. Neither is stealing, murder, or any of the other, quote, sins, unquote."

Puzzled, Gail frowned. "What is the worst?"

"Rejecting God's Son. That's our greatest sin. We're all guilty of a lot of things, Gail. Every single one of us. And yet, when Jesus died he took our sins to the cross with him. It was a gift straight from God. A gift we either accept by asking God's forgiveness, or we reject and continue down the road alone to serve our own punishment in the future. When we accept the price Christ paid for us, we're counted perfect in God's eyes—even though we still slip off the narrow way from time to time."

He waited, then asked, "Are you ready to accept this gift for yourself?"

Drawing in a deep breath, Gail thought about it for a minute. "I'd like to, but.... There are so many things chasing through my mind, I can't sort it all out. At least not enough to make that kind of decision right now."

"I thought not," the pastor replied. "And I'm not about to push you. Just as the decision concerning your baby had to be yours, so must any decision you make about God. It's a personal thing, child."

She felt better on the walk back to the Grants. At least the question of why Pastor Wilkes had not talked to her about becoming a Christian had been answered.

She had been putting off finishing the letter to her baby. Now she decided it was time to get serious. Since withdrawing from school she had the house to herself during the day. And so she sat down to work on the most important theme she would ever write.

Two hours later, after much revision, she at last had on paper the things she wanted her child to know. Carefully she copied it over again on a fresh sheet in her best handwriting. Then she went down to the living room. Standing by the front window in the empty house, Gail read the letter aloud, trying to imagine what she would be feeling if it had been written to her.

To my child,

As I write this you are still so very tiny, all safe and warm inside my body. You will be with me for only another five months, then you will be born to be yourself. I hope they tell me whether you are a boy or a girl.

By now you have been told by the people who adopted you that you were not born to them.

You must wonder who your natural mother and father are and how they could possibly give you up.

Right now I am fifteen. Your father is seventeen. We are both still in high school. I thought we loved each other. But I guess we didn't. At least not enough to spend the rest of our lives together. That's why I'm giving you to a family who can love and care for you. This has not been an easy decision, believe me.

I was born to people who did not want or love me. I'm living now with a foster family. But I want you to belong to a real family. A family all your own.

At first I thought I would keep you. Then I saw it wouldn't work. You need a father as well as a mother. You need adult parents. But please, don't ever think your natural mother—the one carrying you at this moment—rejected you. I am giving you up because I want what is best for you.

It's hard to know what the laws will be by the time you read this. Right now it is legal for someone like me to have an abortion. But I couldn't do that. You have been so real to me from the very first.

I intend to ask your adoptive parents to give this letter to you when you are older. I hope they love you as much as I do. I want you to love them, too. If it's possible, I'd like to think you cared about me just a little, and that you can forgive me for giving you up.

With love—forever and ever,
Your natural mother.

The Sunday after Thanksgiving Gail sat down to reread the letter before placing it in her packed suitcase. Sue would be driving her to the home, seventy miles north of the town where Gail had lived her entire life. While rereading the letter she realized she hardly mentioned Steve. But what could she say? She had no idea how he felt about their child. She couldn't write about how he and his mother wanted her to have an abortion when they first learned she was pregnant. Or that its father cared so little he went to a ball game the night he learned she was pregnant, while his mother came to talk her into an abortion. It made her angry again just thinking about it.

She recalled how quiet Steve had been when he and his father stopped by the week before. Maybe he was hurting, too. Maybe she was not being fair to him. At last Gail swallowed another large chunk of her dwindling pride and called Steve's home.

She breathed a relieved sigh when he was the one who answered the phone. "I just finished packing. Sue's taking the day off from work to drive me to the home tomorrow."

Gail told him then about the letter she had written to their baby, and how she was asking that it be given to the child by its adoptive parents in a few years. "I didn't mention you, other than to give your age and that you were still in high school. Would you like me to add something more about you? Or do you want to write a letter of your own?"

The silence that followed was filled only with a distant hum of the telephone as she waited for Steve to say something other than the "hello" when he answered the telephone.

At last he asked, "What time are you leaving?"

"About nine."

"I'll think about it. I might write something. If you don't hear from me by nine, you'll know I decided not to."

Gail felt numb as she replaced the receiver. Steve had not wished her well or anything. She was left with the feeling she would not see him.

She remained upstairs the next morning until Mack and Ginger left the house. She had told them good-bye the evening before. Mack encouraged her to keep her chin up and not take any guff off anyone. "We'll keep praying for you, Gail. Remember that God loves you and we love you."

Gail was getting ready for bed later when Ginger stopped by her room. She told Gail again she was sorry for the way she continued reacting to her. "I say I'm sorry, and mean it. Then I spout off with something dumb again. I hate myself sometimes," the red-haired girl admitted.

"I know the feeling," Gail replied.

They both grinned and the tension eased. "I hope everything goes okay for you. And for the baby," Ginger added. "No matter what I've said in the past, I think you're pretty brave to do what you're doing. I'd probably have gotten scared and had an abortion to get it over with."

Gail was shaking her head. "No you wouldn't. You're a Christian."

Ginger turned away. "I haven't said this to anyone, but Gail, I don't think I *am* a Christian. I go to church and all that, but there's so much bad stuff inside me. I . . . ." She pushed the door open in mid-sentence and left the room.

The girl's admission really didn't surprise Gail, although she hadn't given it much thought. Ginger had an altogether different attitude than Sue, Mack, or Pastor Wilkes—the only Christians Gail had ever been close to.

The next morning, with breakfast over and the last

minute packing completed, Gail gave up on Steve. The day held no promises under a gray mist-saturated sky. At three minutes before nine she and Sue loaded the suitcases and boxes into Sue's car.

They got in and Sue backed the car from the driveway onto the street. It was then Steve's car rounded the corner. He pulled up in front of them, got out, and walked back to Sue's window. She rolled the glass down and he handed her a folded sheet of paper. Gail took it from Sue without a word.

"Read it and then put my letter with yours," Steve said, leaning down so he could look across at Gail. "I really do want things to go well for you, Gail. And for the baby."

He turned away, glancing back as he headed for his car. "Be seeing you."

Sue and Gail sat there watching as Steve drove off toward the high school. "I don't ever want to see him again as long as I live," Gail spoke with absolutely no emotion left to claim.

10

Lost and Abandoned

Gail held Steve's letter until they reached the freeway and Sue turned the car north. At last she unfolded the paper and began to read. There was no heading. Steve's message to their child began abruptly, with:

> Your mother called last night asking if I wanted her to add something about me in her letter to you. I told her I'd try writing to you myself.
>
> You will soon be adopted by people I know nothing about. Since you won't be reading this until you're older, I hope you'll be able to understand by that time. While I'm your real father I have to admit I don't feel much like it. Your mother has the advantage of being aware of you as you grow inside her. All I feel is an empty nothing.
>
> Now that the decision has been made for you to be put out for adoption, I find I don't care nearly so much about the things that used to be important to me. Your mother is doing the right thing. It's right for you. While I'm glad about that, I'm feeling pretty low down and left out of the decisions right now.
>
> We're too young to get married. We're too young to raise

a baby. It wouldn't work for any of us. Others have done it but they were probably in love. I guess I don't even know what love is, although maybe I'm learning.

If love is the hurt I feel about never seeing you, then I guess I'm at least still human enough to love. Knowing I'll never see you, touch you, or watch you grow, leaves me with an awful emptiness that just won't go away.

Please forgive me for not making it possible for you to be born to your mother and me. I do care about you and will for as long as I live.

Steve's letter ended as abruptly as it had begun with no salutation. Gail took a pen from her purse and added at the bottom: "Love, your father."

The drive to the city where the Salvation Army home was located turned Gail's emotions to dust. She was leaving behind all that was familiar—all she had known her entire life, good and bad. The day was drenched in a feathery mist, shrouding her mood to a dull gray. She sat silent and remote beside Sue as the miles rolled them away to. . . . What?

It took some searching to find the street the home was on once they reached the city. It had been built years before, high above the business and industrial sections on a wooded hillside where large dignified houses aged gracefully among ancient evergreen trees. It seemed a different world. Gail felt as though she was being thrust into a strange new land, although it was only seventy miles from the town where she had been born.

The girl's stomach knotted in tense spasms as Sue maneuvered the car up a twisting street and into the small parking lot. The drive up the hill might have been breathtaking under other circumstances. The yard connecting the red brick six-building complex was neatly trimmed and groomed with an expanse of velvety green between the buildings.

Sue turned the motor off. "It's a pretty place."

"It shouldn't be," Gail noted. "Will giving my baby away be any easier because it's pretty here?"

"It was your decision to come. Try concentrating on what's best for the baby. Think about your own future, too, when this is at last behind you."

Gail slid further down in the seat. "I dread going in there."

"Have you changed your mind? Would you rather remain with us after all? You can, you know."

Gail shook her head.

"We'll be as close as the nearest telephone. Tell you what, why don't you call us collect every day this first week. After that maybe every two or three days. I'll come as often as possible. Pastor Wilkes plans to visit, too.

"Let me share something that works for me, Gail. When I make an effort to help someone through a difficult situation, my own problems tend to heal. Maybe I'm simply getting my mind off myself. Whatever the reason, it works for me. It might for you. Why don't you watch for an opportunity to be a friend to one of these girls? In helping them you just may help yourself."

"Sounds like some kind of Christian gimmick," Gail remarked, a smile tugging at her lips.

Sue laughed. "I guess it is. Jesus said we should help others. I figure if he said it, that's good enough for me. As an added benefit though, you're not only helping that other person, but yourself as well. You can't beat that."

"I guess not. Well...." Gail reached for the door handle. "Let's go on in."

They walked up the steps of the older brick building to a door labeled "Administration Office." Inside the high-ceilinged room they found a scattering of odd chairs in what appeared to be a waiting room. A wide dim hallway led straight back into the building's cavernous depths. A woman welcomed them from behind a desk, then led the way down the long hollow-sounding hall to a small room where a middle aged woman was waiting for them.

She came from around a paper-cluttered table as Sue and Gail entered. "You must be Gail. And you are Mrs. Grant?" the small gray-flecked brunette inquired by way of greeting. "I'm Mary Tripp, one of the social workers here. Let's sit over by the window."

As Gail followed Sue and Mary to a tall narrow window where several chairs were grouped, she wondered about all those other girls who had come before her. What had been their feelings? She wondered, too, about the girl who had been first to enter the home, no doubt baby bloated and scared to death just as she was that very moment. Gail knew times had been different years before when the building was new. People were used to teen pregnancies now, even though they were probably just as hard to face—just as devastating.

She was understanding at last why sex between unmarried people is wrong, and why God planned that children be born into families. Her own recognition of God at that instant surprised her. Yes, she was certain now—for the first time in her life—there was such a Being. She wondered if the outcome might have been different for her if people in general still honored God's intentions about sex. Would she and Steve have acted differently? She wasn't sure. But at least the excuse of, "It won't matter; everyone's doing it," would not have been available as an excuse.

As Gail eased her swelling body into one of the chairs, some of the tension lessened. Mary Tripp appeared to be a caring person. Gail listened as Mary explained the home, what she would find there, and the things that would be expected of her.

"I realize this is a difficult day for you, Gail," she added. "Just remember, those of us here care about you and your baby. We want to help in any way we can. Anytime you have a special problem or concern, you can come to me or the others on staff."

After completing the paperwork, the woman pulled out another sheet and handed it to Gail. On it were a list of rules, printed in detail, along with a map of the complex.

"You may leave now and then, but not without a pass," Mary explained, starting at the top of the page with Gail looking on. "To obtain a pass, you must first finish your class assignments and house duties. Nearly all the girls are given house duties during their stay.

"Classes in the school building are held during the weekdays from nine to three.

"You will be required to go to the dining room at mealtime whether you eat or not. We try to see that each girl receives an adequate diet, and feel if she is sitting at the table during a meal she's more likely to eat even if she thinks she's not hungry."

Mary informed Gail she would have to take care of all adoption procedures away from the home. "It's admirable you intend to release your baby, Gail. But we are not allowed to enter into adoption proceedings. We won't allow a girl to be coerced into, or out of, anything while she's here. We will, however, put you in touch with an adoption agency if you wish."

Sue explained they had already chosen an agency.

All three of them were silent for a few moments as it appeared everything had been said. It was time for Sue to leave. Gail clung to her briefly. "I'll be waiting to hear from you tomorrow, Gail. Don't forget to call." Sue forced a smile. "I'll come as often as I can."

Gail turned back to Mary as Sue left. She felt lost and abandoned. It brought back the panic she had experienced when she was small, and her mother dropped her off at kindergarten for the first time, leaving her alone in a roomful of noisy kids she did not know. Gail's mind raced ahead. Soon the scales would level and tip. Four and a half months from now she would be the one turning and walking way from a child. Her child. Would she actually be able to go through with it? She was not at all sure at that moment.

If Mary had not picked up the suitcases and told Gail to follow with the rest of her things, the girl might have sat down in the middle of the floor and cried, just as she had in that kindergarten classroom at the age of five.

Gail was first shown to her second floor room in one of the two dorms where four neatly made beds were crowded between small desklike tables. The twin-sized beds lined opposite walls, two on one side and two on the other with only three feet separating them in the center. A single window took up the third wall, with the door from the hall and a closet occupying the fourth.

They left Gail's things there, while Mary took her on a tour of the other buildings. There was the school made up of four classrooms, a second dorm, and a dining hall in the basement where the administration offices were housed. A chapel occupied the upper level of the same building. A small infirmary was set apart from the larger structures toward the back.

"The girls are taken to City Hospital when the time comes for their delivery," explained Mary. "They're brought back here twenty-four or so hours later where they usually spend a few days in our infirmary."

Set back behind the infirmary was a small white cottage with a narrow fenced yard. The enclosure was littered with toys.

Gail pointed to it. "Who lives back there?"

"That's our day care center," Mary responded. "The girls can stay on with their babies for up to a year. Others who think they might like to try keeping them, but aren't sure, stay for awhile until they've made up their minds. The babies are cared for in the dorm by their mothers when the girls aren't at school or involved in their house duties."

Gail felt herself growing tense again. So, Lorna had been telling the truth this time. "You mean, mothers with babies actually live right here in the same building with girls like me who have to give theirs away?" she questioned, not willing to believe the truth.

"The same building, yes, but usually not on the same floor," Mary noted. "Those waiting, like you, live on the second floor. Of course, when one or the other becomes crowded we do have to accommodate the overflow." She turned then and walked with Gail back to her dorm.

"Is that a good idea?" Gail questioned. "I mean, letting girls and their babies live here with those of us who have to give ours up?"

"At first I didn't think it was right, either," Mary admitted. "But I've changed my mind. It's a real eye-opener for some, seeing the realities of motherhood first-hand. We on staff provide care and guidance. It's the girls and their babies who provide reality.

"Some girls come to us intending to keep their babies. But after they see the problems, they change their minds. Others, who had planned to relinquish, find themselves unable to let go after all.

"The really sad cases are those who try hanging on to their babies, only to have to give them up after finding their particular situation does not warrant raising a child alone. Some hope the father will come forward, recognizing his responsibilities. But I've found if the father hasn't made provision for the girl and their child before the mother comes here, this seldom happens."

Mary left Gail at the door to her room after pointing

out which bed was hers and the closet she was to use. The fourth bed, Mary told her, was unoccupied at the moment.

It was classtime. The girls were still at the school building, the babies at the cottage day care. How, Gail wondered as she closed the door to the room she would be sharing with two others, would she make it through the next few months? Could she survive here, with girls who were keeping their babies—especially when she wanted hers so badly? Would she be able to hold out—relinquishing her child when the time came? She was not sure. She was not at all sure.

She had just finished unpacking when Mary came to take her to lunch. Before reaching the dining hall they passed a recreation room. Gail was introduced to the other girls during the meal. She guessed there were close to ninety crowded into the small dining room. She met her two roommates there, Margo and Denise. With all the noise and confusion Gail had little chance to do more than mutter a brief hello to the girls she would be rooming with.

Back in the dorm alone, Gail read the rule sheet Mary had given her. She then lay down on her bed to await whatever came next. She supposed it would be the return of her roommates. Gail's apprehension soon eased and she fell asleep.

An outside door banged later as chatter-filled laughter vibrated the halls. It jolted Gail awake. Margo was the first to enter the room. She wore her long brown hair straight. A heavy weariness pinched her sallow features into thin nondescript lines. She tossed her books on the small desk beside her bed that served each occupant as nightstand and study area.

Margo glanced at Gail as she sat on her own bed with a tired sigh. "You're all settled in, I see."

Gail sat up. "I didn't bring much. It's a good thing, I guess, since there's not much room. Have you been here long?"

"Nearly a month," Margo replied with a yawn as she lay back on the bed. "Got another two months to go."

Margo's baby-bulge was evident under her loose shapeless dress. Gail figured the girl to be older than herself by at least three or four years.

Just then the door burst open and Denise swooped in. "Hi!" the petite blond breathlessly greeted her new room-mate.

The girl's appearance shocked Gail. She had not noticed at lunch just how childlike Denise really was. She appeared to be scarcely out of her own baby years with her short straight light brown hair cut in bangs.

The younger girl stopped in front of Gail. "We didn't get a chance to talk at lunch. My baby's going to be born in April. How about yours?"

"Mine, too. Aren't you awfully young to be.... I mean...."

The girl giggled. "I'll be thirteen in six months. People think I'm younger. How old are you?"

"Fifteen," Gail replied. "Have you been here long?"

"I came about the same time as Margo. It's been a month, almost. Girls usually don't come until later in their time. Some wait until just a few weeks before their baby is born. But Mom wanted me out of sight real quick." The girl stopped and grinned knowingly. "Mom's going to make everyone think this is her baby."

Gail glanced at Margo. Their eyes met.

"It gets better. Believe me," Margo intoned. "Go ahead, Denise. Tell her the rest."

The younger girl kicked off her shoes, curling her toes under her as she sat at the end of Gail's bed. "Well, Dad and Mom are divorced. But they still see each other. You know. . . . I mean he comes over and stays all night every once in awhile. Mom told him she got pregnant. She's even wearing a pillowlike thing under her clothes. That way she can raise my baby just like it was hers."

Gail was staring at Denise in disbelief. "You're kidding!"

"No. I'm not. Ya see, my little sister is only two. I'm the oldest. There's four of us kids. When I take this one back to my mom it will make five. We'll get extra welfare money then. It's going to work out just great. I can hardly wait to see what the baby looks like. It's going to be so much fun helping take care of the baby for Mom."

"How does your mother explain you being gone?" Gail questioned.

"Ask her, too," Margo prodded Gail, "how her mother's keeping the secret from Daddy when he comes to visit and decides he wants to spend the night."

"Oh, Mom's got that all worked out," Denise went on, her excitement flushing her rounded childish face. "I'm supposed to be staying with a friend of Mom's in another state. She's saying it's to keep me from the bad influences of my friends. As for Dad, Mom just tells him her doctor said she has to sleep alone till after the baby's born."

Gail did not know what to say. She thought she had come from a mixed-up family situation. But this was something else!

Margo sat up, rubbing her back. "I still say it's not going to work. The welfare—someone—is going to want to see a doctor or hospital record."

The younger girl shrugged. "Mom's taking care of all that."

"How about you, Margo?" Gail asked. "Are you keeping your baby?"

Margo's matter-of-fact tone belied her words. "That's

my business. I'll be eighteen the last of January. No one will have any say then about what I do or don't do. I figure it's nobody's business but mine."

"I'm sorry. I didn't mean. . . ."

Margo reached for a brush and started stroking her long hair. "Hey, no problem. I wasn't trying to put you down. Just wanted to set things straight at the beginning."

11

The Web of Indecision

That evening after dinner in the small lounge at the end of the dorm, Gail met some of the other girls. They accepted her as one of them without question. No one ignored her or turned away. But then, she reasoned, she was not in full retreat now, her main concern being with her baby rather than her own self-consciousness. She felt herself growing more confident as she stopped hiding the awkwardness she usually felt around others.

The girls she met that evening ranged in age from thirteen into their early twenties. Gail learned that the majority were about her own age, somewhere between fourteen and sixteen. All but a few of the older ones attended school there. Some had jobs away from the home during the day. Others were making up classes missed when they dropped out of school.

Gail also learned that two girls with babies shared a room on her floor. Denise explained, "So many are keeping their babies they've had to move them up with us."

The shrill cry of an infant or babble of a toddler, constantly echoed along the halls, seeping under closed doors to reverberate in Gail's heart.

"You'll get used to it," Margo assured her. "Soon you won't notice the noise until it gets quiet—which isn't often."

The next morning Gail opened her eyes to a world of pregnant girls and crying infants. She got up and dressed, then went with the others to the dining room for breakfast. It was her third meal there. When, she wondered, would she begin to feel a part of this strange new world?

Gail met her instructor at the school later. The tall businesslike woman was probably in her fifties. She told Gail they had received her records from her former high school. They felt that with personal help Gail could probably raise her grade level if she was interested.

She was.

That night she made her first collect call to Sue. "I'm doing okay... I guess," she tried to assure the woman. "It's still strange. But most of the people are nice."

On the second day she was given a work assignment. The housemother, Mrs. Howard, came to her room after dinner, taking Gail back to the dining room.

"The girls who are physically able have chores to do each day," the plump, pillow-soft woman explained pleasantly, tucking a stray white curl behind an ear. "I'm going to start you off in the dining room. You'll be working with a couple of other girls.

"You'll be responsible for keeping the tables and floor clean. After breakfast and lunch all you'll need to do is wipe the tables down, and pick up any litter left on the floor. In the evenings, after dinner, the floors have to be swept and mopped. Saturday mornings you'll work a bit harder," she continued with a smile, patting at her hair that kept straying forward along her cheek. "That's when the floors are mopped and waxed and the tables buffed."

The next morning, Wednesday, Gail met the two girls with whom she was assigned to work. One was especially heavy with a soon-due baby, every movement seeming an effort.

She told Gail she had come there the week before. Her baby was expected any day. "At first they weren't going to take me," she remarked. "I guess they don't like us coming just before our babies are born. When I warned them I'd have mine out on the street in front of the place, they changed their minds."

The other girl was not at all talkative, avoiding Gail's every attempt at conversation. Gail decided the quiet one was even more uptight than she. Sue's suggestion, of trying to help someone else, came to mind. But how could she when they completely closed her out?

Gail mentioned the situation to Sue when she talked to her on the phone that night. "Keep yourself open. She might surprise you one of these days and seek you out. That's what I had to do with you."

So far Gail had said nothing to Sue about the situation there—of how some mothers with babies continued living at the home. She knew it would only upset Sue, doing neither of them any good.

As soon as breakfast was over on Saturday morning Gail and her roommates separated to tackle their cleaning chores. After lunch the girls had the rest of the day to themselves. Margo picked up a pass and caught a bus for downtown without a word as to where she was going. Denise had promised to baby-sit for one of the new mothers downstairs and asked Gail if she wanted to go along. Since there was nothing else to do, Gail agreed.

The infant was a girl, barely two weeks old. Gail could not remember ever seeing a baby that tiny. It amazed her, increasing in her the ache to see her own child. Denise, accustomed to helping care for her younger brother and sisters, whipped through a diaper change, then dressed the baby in a new pink outfit she said its mother had made in the home's sewing room.

"You can make all your baby's clothes if you want to," Denise noted. "I don't have to since mom still has lots of things left from us kids. She's hoping this one's a boy. She's got more boy stuff."

Gail could see that even now Denise looked on her baby as belonging to her mother. At last, unable to tolerate the younger girl's dreamworld any longer, she headed back upstairs with the excuse of being tired.

As Gail opened the stairwell door to her floor a curly blond-haired child, barefoot, wearing a diaper and a short blue dress, tottered out from a room. She stopped to stare with wide blue eyes as Gail approached. A girl about Gail's age was lying on a bed inside reading a book. She looked up as Gail hesitated in the open doorway.

"Hi. You must be new."

Gail nodded. "Is this your little girl out here?"

"Yeah. She bothering you?"

"No, I just wondered. She's older than the other babies. Have you been here since she was born?"

"Yep. Thirteen and a half months. They want me to leave. Said they need the room. A year here with your kid is usually the limit."

Gail leaned against the door frame. "Do you have a place to go? I mean a place where you can take her?"

The thin-faced young mother shook her head. "Not yet. I still haven't made up my mind what to do about Amy. My folks say I can't bring her home with me if I go back there. They've made that *real* clear. It looks like I may have to give her up, but it's sure going to be hard after all this time. I'm sort of used to her, you know? Even if she is a brat at times." The last was spoken lovingly, softening the harshness of the words.

Back in her room Gail stood at the window looking out upon the green expanse of lawn and shrubs in winter hue. It was a relief being alone for a few minutes. Silently she resolved to have her mind made up for sure—one way or the other—by the time her baby was born. She did not want to get caught in a web of indecision like the girl down the hall.

It was then she felt the need to talk to someone familiar. Pastor Wilkes came to mind. Dr. Miller had sent money to the home for her use. She had been given a few dollars, including some change, a couple of days before. She rummaged through her purse until she located several quarters, then went out to a pay phone in the hallway.

The pastor sounded pleased to hear from her. He asked how she was getting along and told her he planned to visit soon. "What's the best time of day for you during the week?" he questioned.

Gail told him after school in the afternoons would be best, and he said she could expect him the following Wednesday. Before hanging up he again mentioned he was praying for her. She was glad, although she was not about to admit it.

Sunday morning Gail attended chapel with the other girls. It was said to be mandatory, like having to go to the dining room whether you were hungry or not.

A man in a Salvation Army uniform spoke on giving and receiving. "As you sow," he emphasized, "so shall you reap."

Gail tried to be attentive. She had come quite a ways since first attending church with the Grants. But try as she might she could not latch her mind onto his words.

Then, with chapel nearly over, the man managed to

pierce Gail's daydreams with a suggestion that "You will get out of your stay here at the home just what you are willing to put into it." His words brought to mind Sue's advice the day she left her there. And that reminded Gail of something else. She had not called Sue the day before. Perhaps she was growing accustomed to her new environment after all.

That afternoon, after a quick call to Sue, Gail and two other girls picked up passes and caught a bus to a shopping mall. It was good to get away from the home for a while and see that the world was still intact on the outside. They walked around and looked at things. Gail bought them all a hamburger, deciding she might as well spend some of the doctor's money.

On Monday, after being at the home a full week, Gail learned the girls still awaiting the birth of their babies attended childbirth classes. Most chose the natural birth method. Gail was not sure if that was for her or not. Did she really want to see her baby born if she could not keep it? And yet since it was the class the majority were taking, she went along with the others.

Wednesday seemed like it would never come. At last, on Wednesday afternoon, Mary Tripp sent Gail word that a visitor waited to see her. Wearing jeans and a loose fitting shirt, Gail hurried to the administration building, entering from the back. Her heels sent a hollow ring echoing along the hall as she hurried toward the visitor's lounge.

The pastor waited in the large room across from Mary's office. Some chairs and a couple couches were grouped here and there around the room allowing the girls and their visitors a degree of privacy. A girl from the other dorm was there with a man and woman Gail guessed were her parents.

Pastor Wilkes stood looking up at a picture on the wall, his hands clasped behind him, his back to the door. He turned when she entered, his easy smile alighting comfortably across his wide face. "Gail!" He crossed with a long stride to give her a hug. "So," he held her at arm's length, "let me look at you. Tell me, do you like it here?"

"It's okay, I guess. Some of the girls are a little strange. But then they probably think I'm strange." She grinned, then turned serious. "The hardest part is having so many girls living here with their babies. Especially when I can't keep mine. But, for the most part—it's okay."

"I didn't know they allowed mothers to remain after their babies were born," he noted.

Gail explained the situation, as it had been related to her, then told him about her two roommates. While he did not appear shocked to learn someone Denise's age was pregnant, he did register sadness over the younger girl's situation.

"And what about you, Gail? Have you had opportunity to think how the Lord might fit into your life?"

"Well . . ." she began, "I feel there *is* a God now. I'm just not sure he cares about me. If he did, why would he let me be born to a mother who didn't love or want me?"

"That wasn't the Lord's doing, Gail. It was a direct result of your mother's rebellion."

Later, before he left, he prayed for her and her baby again as he had before she came to the home. He also prayed for the couple—whoever they might be—who were to adopt her child. Gail walked out to the hallway with the pastor as he left.

The other girl's parents were leaving too, and so she and Gail walked back toward their dorms together. "Your grandfather seemed nice," the girl remarked.

"That wasn't my grandfather," Gail told her. "That was my pastor." As they separated Gail realized what she had said. "*my* pastor." Well, she decided, he was.

On Friday evening Sue and Ginger came to the home,

and once again Gail was called to the visitor's lounge. Sue ran to meet her as soon as Gail entered the room, grabbing her tight for a second. "Honey, are you all right?"

Gail smiled and nodded, then glanced at Ginger. She wished the redhead had not come. "Hello, Ginger."

The girl came closer. "I thought I'd better come with Mom this time. She was pretty torn up after bringing you here."

Sue appeared embarrassed. "It was just that I could see how frightened you were," she explained to Gail. "There seemed to be nothing I could do to help since you insisted on coming."

They sat in a semicircle with Gail and Sue facing one another and Ginger between them to one side.

"I was scared," Gail admitted. "But I think the worst is over—at least until I have to sign my baby away." Gail told them then about the girls who continued living there with their babies.

Sue eyes registered genuine shock. "You don't mean you all live here together, do you?"

Gail nodded. "That's what I mean. I was pretty upset at first. I was going to tell you when we talked on the phone, but I didn't want to worry you until I was sure I could handle it."

"It must be terribly difficult for those of you who have to give your babies up. I wish they had mentioned this to us before you came," Sue said.

Gail told them, too, about the girl who had been there for over a year, and who was now facing the possibility of having to give her baby up. Glancing down at her hands, Gail noticed they were trembling. What was happening to her? She thought she had things together. And now. . . .
A warm tear splashed on the end of her thumb. Quickly she wiped it away.

"It must be awful for you," Ginger declared, with what

appeared to be genuine sympathy.

The quiet tears into a torrent of sobs. "It's just that . . . that I . . . I want my baby so much. When I see girls like her, though, and remember . . . remember Jill back home, I know it's . . . it's impossible."

At last Gail regained some control and blew her nose. After that it was impossible to convince Sue and Ginger she was really all right. "Must be my condition or something," she remarked with as casual a grin as she could manage.

Sue was obviously still upset when she and Ginger left sometime later. Even Ginger seemed distraught, offering, "If you ever want to come back home, Gail, it's okay with me."

Gail shook her head. "Thanks. But I'd better stay here."

She was angry with herself after they left. She hadn't realized how close to the edge she was balanced until her feelings crumbled. It took awhile, but she finally managed to pull herself together again, calling Sue as soon as she figured she and Ginger had reached home. Gail apologized for upsetting them, trying once again to convince Sue she really was just fine.

Another weekend slipped by. On Tuesday night the dorm came alive with excitement. Nancy, one of the girls down the hall, had gone into labor and was taken to City Hospital. Although Gail did not know Nancy very well, she found herself as caught up in the suspense as the others. The small lounge at the end of the first floor filled with girls after dinner, awaiting word from the hospital. The girl Gail had talked to—the one who would soon be leaving—was there with her daughter Amy. A couple of the girls sat on the floor rolling a ball back and forth to the child who giggled and tottered after it. Gail watched Amy's mother, trying to guess what she was thinking.

As the chatter increased, Margo asserted herself. "Oh, calm down!" she urged, as several appeared on the verge of talking themselves into an anxiety attack over the possibilities of all that could go wrong. "Nancy may be in labor for hours," Margo told them. "The baby might not even be born tonight."

A dark-haired girl groaned. "You're such a cheerful soul, Margo. Why don't you go on back to your room if you don't care about Nancy or her baby."

Margo's usual deadpan expression snapped to life. "Don't accuse *me* of not caring! Not after the way you've badgered her. That goes for all of you who've kept your babies, or are planning to." Margo glanced around the room. "You haven't given Nancy a single day of peace since she told you she was relinquishing her baby."

"We just wanted to keep her from making a mistake," a second girl remarked. "Just because you don't want yours, and plan to give it away, is no reason to act so smug. But then, maybe it's right for you. Who'd want *you* for a mother."

Gail was about to come to Margo's defense when her roommate leaned back with a sudden calm and smiled. "You have no idea what I intend to do. None of you know. Just because I don't go around baring my soul the way the rest of you Wailing Winnies do gives you no right to think you know me or my plans."

Anger stirred the crowded room as tempers and accusations heated. Amy fretted. Someone tossed a tattered magazine across the room. Through it all Margo just sat there with an irritating smile of self-satisfaction.

It was the phone ringing in the hall that finally cooled the rising heat of emotion. Three girls closest to the door ran to answer it. Talk hushed as the others waited to see if it was news about Nancy. Amy's mother reached down and quietly pulled the now sleepy child into her arms, rocking back and forth, holding the toddler close. As she brushed the curly locks from the child's forehead and kissed it, a lump swelled in Gail's throat.

At last the girls who had gone to answer the phone returned. The tallest one, June, made the awaited announcement. "Nancy delivered an eight-pound boy forty-five minutes ago. They're both fine."

A whoop went up from the group as Gail felt a surge of elation. Margo was the only one who appeared gloomy.

"There's more," June said, raising her voice so she could be heard again.

The room chatter died.

"Nancy's already signed adoption papers."

Silence chilled the group. Slowly, one by one, the girls left the room. Gail glanced at Margo who remained seated. She seemed even more depressed than before. As Gail was about to leave, she stopped, looking back at her roommate. "Are you coming?"

"It's rotten!" Margo exploded now that they were alone. "It's a rotten, creepy world! There's nothing but hurt, pain, and suffering. The guys get away with whatever they want. We're the ones who suffer—and our children. Where do you suppose the father of Nancy's baby is tonight? What do you figure he's doing right now while she separates herself forever from her child who's been a part of her for the last nine months?" Margo glared at Gail as though it was her fault. "Nancy loved her baby, you know!"

Gail was taken back by Margo's outburst. "I didn't know Nancy that well. But Margo, we're to blame, too. It's not just the guys' fault."

Margo stood up. "Nancy loved that baby from the minute she knew she was pregnant. Now she's had to give it up."

"I thought you probably felt she was doing right letting

it go. I mean, by the way you were talking a few minutes ago...."

Margo walked to the door. "You don't know how I feel about anything, Gail. None of you do. So don't try outguessing me."

With a toss of her head Margo swept her long hair back, resuming her former composure. Then she straightened her thin shoulders, and opened the door. Her head high, her lips stretched into a slight smile, Margo left Gail standing alone in the empty room.

Gail realized she had just been given a glimpse of the real Margo—the one the girl tried so hard to keep hidden. For a few brief moments Gail had peered behind the mask. And then, before her eyes, she watched Margo slip back into character.

12

Hurt Begets Hurt

There were times when Gail felt a sense of rightness about giving her baby up for adoption. At other times she could see nothing ahead for her and her child except a lifetime of regret no matter what direction she chose. Could she do as Nancy had? Would she be strong enough? Could she relinquish—actually cast her own child from her into the arms of strangers who would become not only its mother and father, but later the grandparents of her very own child's children? She was just not sure.

Some of the girls tried pinning Gail down on her plans regarding her baby. But she decided to follow Margo's example, keeping the decision to herself. She told them only that she had not made up her mind. It was certainly no lie. The pressure from the other girls living there with their babies was constant. She could see both sides of the situation. There were times when a baby was simply angelic, melting even Margo's guarded heart. At other times, when a child became demanding, changing into something more akin to a fallen angel, Gail was positive she was right in giving hers up.

Gail wished Lorna could spend a few days with her there. She would soon have her eyes opened. A baby was not a possession automatically offering unconditional love and companionship to its mother. Babies had needs—needs most of the younger mothers seemed incapable of supplying as they struggled through their own maturing.

It was toward the last of the second week when a new girl moved into the room Gail shared with Margo and Denise. Janet, at twenty-five, was older than any of the others. "Hope you don't mind sharing space with a black girl," Janet greeted Denise and Gail as the two returned from class that afternoon.

The color of Janet's skin did not bother Gail. But her obvious maturity did. She was tall, radiating a bright smile when the occasion called for it. It was not long before Gail decided the atmosphere in their room would definitely benefit from Janet's presence. Margo's gloom, countered by Denise's endless childish chatter, was getting to Gail. Janet would help balance out the two extremes.

She noticed a gold band on the third finger of Janet's left hand as Denise inquired, and found out, that their new roommate expected her baby in May.

Janet glanced down at her hand when she noticed Gail's attention focused on the ring. "It's for real. I am . . . or I should say, I was married. I still consider myself Michael's wife." She twisted the gold band on her finger. "He was killed by a hit and run driver while walking across the street on his way to work a couple months ago. It was just after we learned I was pregnant with our first child."

"Oh.... I'm sorry," Gail offered.

Janet smiled. "It's probably unusual for someone my age to come here, especially when I'm carrying my husband's baby. But we had no insurance for that kind of accident, and neither of our families were able to help. Since I was in no condition to go out looking for work, it was suggested I come here until my baby is born and I'm able to find a job."

With Christmas fast approaching Gail went downtown to shop for some inexpensive gifts for Sue, Mack, and Ginger. She bought her mother, Beverly Richards, a cosmetic case and mailed it without including a return address, then picked up some items for her three roommates.

Sue's next visit was on Christmas Eve. She came loaded down with brightly wrapped packages on the afternoon of Christmas Eve for Gail and the three who shared her room. There were homemade cookies and candy. And from Pastor Wilkes, there was a Bible for Gail. The Grants had invited her for Christmas, but Gail turned them down. Once more Sue asked if Gail might not reconsider.

Again Gail declined. "I really think it's best if I stay here," she told the woman. "Going back now would only make it harder. Besides, I don't want to chance running into Steve or his parents."

Gail did not know what to expect of Christmas at the home. She was pleasantly surprised when it turned out to be the best Christmas ever. The girls who did not go home got together to cook a special meal for themselves in the big kitchen, ending the day with an old-fashioned taffy pull instigated by Janet.

That night, probably as a result of all the food and sweets she had eaten, Gail awoke with indigestion. The doctor who regularly came to the home had given her some antacid when she first complained of discomfort. She got up quietly, trying to keep from waking the others, and took the medication. By that time she was wide awake and so decided to slip downstairs to the lounge to read for a while.

Gail was surprised to find two other girls already there. Connie sat smoking at the far end of the room as though her life depended upon each drag, a blanket snugged around her shoulders. Smoking inside the building was not permitted, but Gail was not about to point that out after noting the sullen determination chiseled across Connie's face. Terri, wrapped in a blue bathrobe, sat by herself close to the door leafing through a ragged periodical. The silence in the room was broken only by the ruffling pages.

"I thought I'd be the only one up," Gail noted, easing her expanding bulk into an overstuffed chair. "I think I ate too much. But it was all so good."

Terry glanced up, her tawny-toned hair curling softly about her face. "I missed not being home. But I just couldn't go. I'm not up to facing people on the outside yet."

"Me either," Gail agreed, understanding perfectly.

"Christmas is for merchants, dummies, and kids," Connie intoned.

Connie and Terri were roommates and both of their babies were due soon. Gail had become better acquainted with them over the holiday. Terri was usually quiet and reserved, while Connie always appeared to be mad at someone or something.

Terri pushed the magazine aside. "Kim, our roommate, went into labor awhile ago. They've taken her to the hospital."

Connie's long black hair—obviously dyed—had been permed into a frizzed mass of various length curls, giving her a wild look. Her white complexion was highlighted with heavy black eyebrows and lashes. Gail wondered if Connie's mannerisms weren't designed to fit the image she was evidently trying to project. Whatever the reason, the girl's sullenness flashed a constant warning.

"I was supposed to deliver this month, too," she complained, taking another long drag from her cigarette. "Now it looks as though the brat's going to hold off on me until after the first of the year."

"There's still a few days left in the month," Gail offered.

Connie ground out her stub and reached for another. "This month or next—it really doesn't matter much." She smiled. "All that's really important is that they're finally going to pay through the nose!"

Gail wanted to ask who "they" were, but she caught a warning glance from Terri.

"Want to hear my plans?" Connie asked, leaning forward.

"If you want to tell me," Gail replied with some hesitation.

"Sure. Why not! Ya see, I've got this ultrarespectable family. Dad's a lawyer. Mom volunteers all over the place. Anyone who needs a hand with something calls on good old Mom and she's right there. After they had me they decided they didn't want any more kids.

"As soon as I was old enough I was given household chores. Before long it was, 'Connie, have dinner ready by six'. Or, 'Connie, see that the floors are clean and the laundry finished by the time I get home from my meeting.' When I got older I wondered why we didn't hire help the way some of Mom's friends did. Then I saw that Mom didn't need hired help as long as she had me!"

Terri shook her head with a slight shudder. "It couldn't have been as bad as all that. You *do* have a tendency to exaggerate."

"Oh, yeah? How would you know? You're always bragging about your folks. How would you know what someone like me has had to put up with?"

"I just know my parents care about me," Terri said. "And I'll bet yours do too. I can't imagine anyone using their daughter like that."

"I don't know, Terri," Gail put in. "I haven't had it so easy myself. You can't always tell what other people are like."

"See." Connie leaned forward pointing at Gail, but directing her comment to Terri. "Gail understands. Anyway," she turned back to Gail, "I'm finally going to get even with them. My dad believes everyone should be made to pay for their actions. I think he probably intends to be a judge someday.

"Anyway, when he found out I was pregnant, he said I had to keep the kid. I think he figures it will teach me a lesson. Mom said they'd set me up in an apartment and pay all the bills until I'm out of high school and go through some kind of vocational training. Dad's even planning to hire a baby-sitter until I can get a job.

"At first I thought I'd just go ahead and have an abortion. But then I decided, no, why not go along with them. At least to a point. I'll be eighteen in six months. And the very next day—the day after my birthday, I'm dropping this kid off at grandpa and grandma's house and taking off like a bird."

Connie's face flushed as she warmed to the telling. "That's another thing. Mom's going bananas already over becoming a grandmother. I wish I had enough time to teach the kid to call her granny before I leave." She rocked back in her chair, laughing as the thought tantalized her imagination. "Wouldn't that be a blast!" She sobered when she found neither Gail nor Terri enjoying the joke.

"It's disgusting," Terri muttered under her breath, "using a baby like that."

"Listen, Miss High and Mighty. You said your family expects you to keep your baby when you don't want to. You're no better off than me."

"I don't plan to get even with anyone!" Terri countered.

Connie jumped up, snuffing out her cigarette. "I'm going to bed. The company here is getting dull."

As Connie scuffed out of the lounge, Terri leaned her head back, staring up at the ceiling. "She's so full of bitterness. There's just no talking to her. I've tried, but I can't get through." The girl sighed, putting a hand on her protruding stomach. "But then, who am I to be offering advice?"

"I can't believe she really intends to do that. Connie's probably just spouting off," Gail suggested, hoping she was right.

Terri was shaking her head. "I don't know. She's built up a lot of resentment. My folks do want me to keep my baby, but they aren't insisting on it the way Connie says her parents are.

"Mom and Dad are Christians. I...." Terri turned away. "I'm ashamed to admit it, but I'm a Christian, too. I mean, I'm ashamed to be a Christian in this kind of mess. My parents want me to bring the baby back home so they can help care for it while I finish high school. They wanted me to stay home and have the baby there. But I just couldn't. I'm still not sure I'm going to keep it."

"You're lucky," Gail commented with obvious envy. "The only ones who care anything about me are the Grants, the foster parents I was living with, and the minister where they go to church. They feel I'm too young to try to raise my baby, and if they do anything to help me keep it they'll just be adding a second mistake to the one I've already made. But I'd still give anything—just anything—if I didn't have to relinquish this baby."

Terri moved uncomfortably in her chair. "I really don't want my baby, Gail. I suppose that sounds awful to you. But I want to go on to college. I'm not ready to be a mother."

Gail could not help smiling. "Well, as they say, ready or not...."

Blushing slightly, Terri confided, "I'm thinking seriously about relinquishing it to a family who can support it the way a child should be supported. Not only with money, but with whatever it is I don't have at this stage of my life."

"You have your parents to back you," Gail offered by way of protest.

Sorrow darkened Terri's eyes. "The main problem, I guess, is I don't want to be pregnant, or an unmarried mother at seventeen."

Gail related her own misgivings about giving up the baby she wanted so much to keep. "If we could only exchange places. I want my baby, and yet there's no way I can keep it. You want to give yours up when you could keep it. Doesn't seem fair, does it?"

The two talked for a while then went back to their own rooms. A bond had been formed during that early morning vigil there in the lounge. Gail wished Terri was not so close to delivering so they could get to know one another better. There was something about her. Gail couldn't put a tag on what it was. She wondered, did it have anything to do with Terri claiming to be a Christian?

This gave Gail even more reason for reflection. She had felt she wasn't good enough for God to accept. But here Terri openly admitted she was a Christian and yet she was pregnant. While it didn't make a lot of sense, it did cause Gail to think. Maybe she had a chance after all—*if* she should ever decide to claim Christianity for herself.

Two weeks later Connie's baby was born. A week after that she and her infant son left the home for an apartment her parents had set up for them. The birth of her baby had done nothing to change Connie's plans. According to Terri, Connie's last words before leaving were, "Boy, will my folks be steamed when I dump little Joey off at Granny and Gramps' house six months from now."

The afternoon after Connie and her son departed Gail was called to the visitor's lounge. She had been expecting Pastor Wilkes. He had already paid her two visits and was due to come again. She hurried across to the administration building that damp Tuesday, to find not the pastor, but her mother watching for her at the door of the lounge.

Gail stopped in shocked surprise. "I didn't expect it would be you," she said not knowing what sort of greeting to offer. It did not appear as though her mother had been drinking, at least not enough to show. "Want to sit down? Looks like we've got the place to ourselves."

Beverly Richards remained where she was. The black haired woman was dressed in tan slacks and a brown imitation fur jacket. "The baby's really showing, isn't it?" Her voice betrayed her evident shock at seeing her daughter in that condition.

Gail nodded. "It should be. I'm six months along."

"How do you like this place? Are they treating you good?"

"It's okay. How did you find me?"

"I sure didn't learn where you were from you, did I? You didn't even put a return address on the package you sent for Christmas." Beverly observed. She raised her hand to stop any rebuttal Gail might be ready to fire back. "I know. I know. I guess I didn't deserve to hear from you at all. Not after the things I said the last time we saw each other. I shouldn't have put the blame on you. I know it's not your fault I got pregnant, or that it destroyed my marriage."

Not knowing what to say, Gail chose to say nothing.

"I've been doing a lot of thinking since you came to see me at work," the woman went on. "I'm sorry for not being the sort of mother I should have been to you. I'd like to try to make up for the past."

"Mom, I can understand how you must have felt. I don't hold things against you like I did. After all, I'm no better."

Beverly took her daughter's arm and led her over to some chairs so they could sit down. The woman leaned forward with an intensity Gail had never before seen in her mother. "Just listen to me for a minute, Gail. I called and talked to Mrs. Grant. She told me where you were and that you were planning to give your baby up. She said you didn't want to at first, but that you'd changed your mind. Gail, would you still like to keep your baby? I mean, if I took you home with me?"

Gail stared at her mother. "I was taken away from you, remember? I'm still a ward of the court."

Avoiding Gail's eyes, Beverly suggested, "I think I might be able to talk them into letting you come back with me. They wanted me to make some changes before but I wasn't willing at the time." She looked directly into Gail's dark eyes. "I'd like another chance, Gail. I'll even go to a place to dry out, this time for good. I promise."

Gail stood up, walking to the window that faced her dorm. How many times had her mother promised to stop drinking? It was an old story by now. How could she take a baby into the sort of environment she had been wrenched from? "It wouldn't work," Gail spoke at last. "We've never been close. The baby would end up in the middle, making us all miserable."

Beverly got to her feet as Gail turned back from the window. "You don't trust me to stay sober."

Gail did not answer, but her silence told the story.

"I need you, Gail," her mother pleaded, tears streaking her mascara. "I need you and your baby. Aaron has gone to live with his father. I hardly ever see him anymore. I'm all alone now. Really alone. . . ."

Gail wanted to ask about her mother's men friends who had been underfoot during the time she had lived at home. But she didn't. Pity swept her. And yet, she had to think of her baby first, and the life it would have with the two of them. Gail did not feel she could trust her. She hoped her mother was sincere, but it was too soon to tell.

"I can't," Gail finally told her.

Throwing up her hands, Beverly declared, "Well! I tried!"

Gail followed her mother to the door. "I'm grateful for the offer. Honest. It means a lot to me. It's just that I don't think it would work for either of us, or for the baby."

The woman faced her daughter when she reached the door, hurt and anger sweeping her once carefully made up face, now streaked and damp.

"You see," Gail tried to explain, "I want my baby to have a father and a mother. It's important to me. Can you understand that?"

"Yes," Beverly responded, sadness edging her voice. "Only too well."

Gail smiled. "You really don't want people to start calling you grandma, do you?"

The still trim attractive woman yielded with a pained smile. "Oh, I don't know. . . . It might not be so bad."

Her tone and words touched Gail. "Someday, Mom, when I'm older and married, you can be grandma to my kids. And that's a promise."

13

An Unexpected Visitor

Sue came to the home on the Saturday following Beverly Richards' visit. "I thought you might need to talk after seeing your mother," she explained as she and Gail sat across from each other at a downtown restaurant.

It did help to talk about her mother's offer. "As much as I'd like to believe it would work, I just can't," Gail concluded.

Sue observed that if her mother were unable to stop drinking or change her lifestyle, Gail would be locked right back into the same situation from which she had escaped. Only this time there would be another child— her child—to consider.

While Gail knew Sue was right, it did nothing to ease the ache of wanting to keep the son or daughter she would bear but never know. Deciding something in her mind was far easier than letting go with her heart. It was impossible not to wonder from time to time if it might not work to take her baby back to her mother's.

Gail missed Terri after the girl's baby was born. They had grown close in the short time they had before the baby's birth. They had enjoyed a quiet New Year's Eve with some of the other girls, and had spent several long evening hours alone just talking.

Before her release from the home, Terri asked to see Gail. She was in a room at the home's infirmary with her baby when Gail walked in.

"When I saw him I couldn't resist," Terri said. "I told them I wanted to hold him. I wanted to see if I felt anything special. And, Gail, I did. I do! It's as though God pressed a button somewhere and turned on all my mothering instincts." Terri's young face radiated through the joyful tears that dampened her cheeks.

Gail was happy for her. And yet it only deepened her own sadness. Her mothering instincts were already in full bloom with no satisfactory opportunity to yield to them.

It was the last Sunday in February when Gail awoke to find Margo's bed empty. Her suitcase, the one that had been packed and ready for the hospital, was also gone.

Gail got up and went to Janet's bed, gently shaking her awake. "Did you see Margo leave?" she whispered.

Janet rolled over and stretched, then glanced around. "No. Did she go into labor?"

"I don't know. I just woke up and saw she was gone. So is her suitcase."

Denise was tangled in her blankets when Gail woke her. "Did you see Margo leave?"

The younger girl shook her head sleepily, then opened her eyes wider. "Is Margo's baby coming?"

"I have a feeling it is. I wonder why she didn't tell us."

"You know Margo," Janet reminded them, sitting up and reaching for her robe. "That girl is the most secretive person I've ever known."

As the three left their room together to try to find what had happened, they met Mrs. Howard coming toward them down the hallway. "Yes," she told them, "Margo woke me about two hours ago. She's already been taken to the hospital. Evidently she was in labor for several hours and didn't tell anyone until she felt she had to. I just called the hospital. They told me it would probably take some time yet."

Late that night Margo was still in labor. Gail and Janet remained in the lounge alone to await word while Denise went on to bed, secure in her happily-ever-after illusion Margo would have a healthy baby by the time she awoke the next morning. At last Janet and Gail gave up, too. Monday morning the story was the same with Margo still in labor.

"They give her stuff so it won't hurt, don't they?" Denise questioned as the three dressed for breakfast.

Janet glanced at the girl and then at Gail. "It hurts. They help all they can though."

When the three returned from breakfast they found a note taped to their door. It was from Mary Tripp. She wanted to see them right away. They hurried off together figuring it had to be about Margo. Gail was suddenly afraid of what Mary had to tell them. A birth was usually announced to everyone.

They found Mary in the administration building. "Is it about Margo?" Denise asked breathless as the three swooped down on the woman.

Mary nodded. "The baby didn't make it. Margo is exhausted, but she's going to be all right. She wanted me to tell you three first. She didn't have many friends here."

Gail touched her own stomach. Margo's baby was dead? It seemed unreal. Margo had been just like the rest of them two days ago. She had chosen to give her child life rather than abort it. Now, after coming to the home and carrying her baby through nine long months, Margo's child was as dead as if it had been aborted at the very beginning. It didn't seem fair.

"Will she be coming back here?" Janet asked.

"I'm not sure. Right now she's not able to be moved," Mary told them.

"Was her baby a boy or a girl?" Denise inquired in a voice scarcely above a whisper. "I always thought Margo would have a boy." The girl's usual innocent exuberance stilled as reality hung over them.

"It was a boy," Mary responded.

Gail struggled through the rest of the day in a fog. That night she and Janet asked permission to go visit Margo at the hospital. But they were told their former roommate had requested there be no visitors.

A few days later Margo's belongings were removed from their room. Mrs. Howard explained that Margo was going directly home from the hospital with her parents who had come to take her back to Florida.

"She never once mentioned her parents, or where she was from," Janet remarked.

Gail nodded. "None of us knew anything about her. Now we'll never know what she planned for herself or her baby."

The next day a new girl moved in to take Margo's place. Joyce was fourteen but in some ways seemed younger than Denise. While Denise was bubbly, Joyce pouted, exhibiting an "I want things my own way or else" air.

She answered Denise's perpetual question by telling them her baby was due the last of March. "I hate the way I look," the girl asserted. "I hate feeling and looking like the Goodyear Blimp." Joyce was well rounded in places other than her baby bulge. Her short hair, cut in harsh layers, had been bleached sun yellow sometime back, the dark roots now showing through.

"You've only got a month more to go," Janet consoled half-heartedly.

"Yeah. I was supposed to get to stay home through it all, but my folks decided to ship me off here at the last minute. I hate this dump. It's like a prison."

Gail could well understand the girl's parent's decision to "ship her off," if she was like this at home.

"I was going to have an abortion when I first learned this thing," Joyce looked down at her round stomach, "had started growing in me. Then I decided no one was going to take a part of *me* away and throw it in a garbage can. My brothers and sisters have been taking my things all my life. This is something that's *all* mine." She sighed. "I just didn't think I'd get this big!" Joyce sat on the edge of her bed and bent forward. "Look. I can't even reach my feet anymore."

"What'd you expect?" Janet asked in disgust. "A picnic?"

Joyce giggled. "No, but that's where it all started."

Janet turned away. "Oh, please, spare us the details."

"Are you going to keep your baby?" Denise asked timidly.

Joyce shrugged. "I may. I may not. I don't know yet. Depends on what it looks like."

Gail shuddered and made an excuse about having to go see someone about something. Joyce's raw vocal stabs cut deep after what had happened to Margo. Gail, Denise, and Janet were still grieving over Margo's loss, drawing the three of them close. To have someone like Joyce thrown in with them now. . . . It was just too much.

Gail told Sue during her next visit about Margo and all that had happened. A few days later she received a long letter from Pastor Wilkes. He included some verses he suggested she look up in the Bible he had given her for Christmas. She found a couple of them, but gave up looking for the rest since he explained them all in his letter anyway. It was a good letter, and it did help some.

On the third day after Joyce moved to the home she confided to Gail that she intended to slim her baby down. "It's getting way too big. I'm putting little old fatso on a diet as of today."

Gail tried talking her out of it, and was about to go find Mrs. Howard, when Joyce threatened to do something even worse if Gail didn't promise to keep her secret. And so Gail was forced to watch as Joyce chased her food around her plate at every meal for two days, eating very little, scraping the rest into a paper bag she carried with her to the dining room.

Two days later Gail returned to their room to find Joyce alone. She was standing in front of the open closet repeatedly bumping her protruding stomach against the door edge.

"What do you think you're doing now!" Gail demanded.

"I'm tired of looking like this," the girl complained. "I don't want to have to lug this thing around another whole month. I want it to get out right now—today."

Gail yanked Joyce away from the door, shoving her down to the bed. "I'm going to report you. You could hurt your baby. Don't you care about anything or anyone but yourself?"

"No!" Joyce shot back.

Gail stood over the girl, her dark eyes ablaze. "Margo, the girl who used that bed before you came, lost her baby when it was born. She carried it for nine whole months, and then it died. I won't let that happen to your baby. Not if there's anything I can do to stop it. Do you understand!"

Joyce's rebellion subsided. "You don't have to get so mad. You're the only friend I've got here."

That evening Janet found Gail in the dining room

showing two new girls the evening cleanup routine. Janet called Gail off to one side. "Joyce passed out in the bathroom. They've taken her to the hospital. She may have her baby early."

A cold chill gripped Gail. "It's not due for another month. I should have reported it when I found her trying to beat her baby to death. If she's killed the baby it's going to be my fault."

"Honey," Janet said, her dark face revealing her concern as she put an arm across Gail's shoulders, "you've been trying to help her. We're uptight right now after what's happened to Margo."

Gail went to find Mrs. Howard later, to tell her all that Joyce had been doing. The woman said they were aware Joyce had limited her food intake, but had hoped she would decide to eat again on her own.

Before they went to bed that night Mrs. Howard come to the girls' room to tell them Joyce had had her baby. "It's a good size for eight months. Over six pounds." She turned to Gail. "You needn't worry anymore. The baby is healthy. It's a girl. My guess is Joyce was closer to having it than either she or the doctor thought."

The next morning Gail awoke early with a dull cramp down low, and a stabbing backache. It had been months since she'd experienced period cramps. She went to the bathroom and found a trace of blood. Fright seized her. First Margo, then Joyce, and now her.... She woke Janet and asked her to find Mrs. Howard. Then she lay back on her bed as Denise fussed over her, obviously frightened.

The woman came and checked on Gail while Denise watched in silence. Janet was holding the younger girl, who was by then sobbing, as the ambulance medics took Gail away. Before many minutes passed Gail was settled into a room at City Hospital. Tests were taken and she was given a shot of some kind. The doctor ordered Gail to remain in bed. She was not even allowed bathroom privileges. By afternoon the cramps had subsided, but there was still a slight show of blood and her back continued to hurt.

Somehow Joyce learned Gail was at the hospital and came to her room that afternoon. She said she was leaving to go back to the home yet that evening. "I had a girl," she announced with obvious pride. "I think she's pretty."

"I heard about it," Gail said.

"Are you going to lose your baby?"

Gail longed for Joyce to just go away and leave her alone. "I hope not."

"Why not? It would all be over for you if you did."

"I want my baby to live—to grow up and be somebody. I love my baby, and care what happens to it."

Joyce shrugged. "Well, so do I. I'm keeping mine, you know. Did they tell you?"

Taking a deep breath, Gail steeled herself. "Will your parents let you take her back home with you?"

"I'll stay at the Salvation Army place for a while. After my folks see how much I want it, I'm sure they'll let me."

Joyce was still referring to her baby daughter as an "it." Before their babies were born most of them—Gail included—thought about their babies as its. But not afterward.

"You don't know what you're getting into," Gail told her.

Joyce turned to leave. "It's mine and no one's going to take it away from me. Not ever!"

Gail was relieved when Joyce finally left. She didn't need the added upset at this point in her pregnancy.

A nurse came to tell Gail the doctor wanted her to remain in the hospital for a few days. She was comforted to know that he felt her baby had a good chance if she was careful.

The Grants were notified and Sue and Mack came that evening. It was the first time Mack had come with Sue. He ruffled Gail's hair and asked, "What are you doing, girl? Trying to scare us?" The man turned serious then. "Are you and the baby going to be all right? What did the doctor say?"

Sue was shaking her head. "My, aren't you becoming the little mother hen."

Looking sheepish, Mack held his hands in front of him, palms up. "Hey, I care about this girl. Okay?"

Putting her arm around his middle, Sue sighed. "It's very much okay. But it's going to puncture your image if you don't watch out."

Gail giggled. It was the first time she had felt at ease with Mack. This was the way he and Ginger carried on at times.

"Besides," he was continuing, "we've got a lot to thank Gail for."

"Thank me? For what?"

"For helping set Ginger on track again. Your situation has made her do some serious thinking. Home seems a pretty good place to her now, since learning what you've had to go through."

Sue was nodding. "Ginger has been talking with Pastor Wilkes. I think she's about to make an important decision about her relationship to the Lord."

After the Grants left, Gail lay there thinking about the things they had said. It was about time Ginger appreciated what she had.

Gail realized she was bothered less about her own mother's lack of nurturing skills as she looked more and more to Sue for strength and support. Now she and Mack had worked through the awkwardness that had stood between them. If things were different she could probably be happy living with them again.

The next afternoon as Gail was lying in bed watching a game show on the overhead television, she caught a glimpse of someone standing in the open doorway. She turned her head then froze. . . .

"Hello, Gail."

It was Steve.

"How—how did you know? I mean, who told you I was here?"

"Ginger. At school this morning. She said you almost lost the baby."

"If I stay in bed, and do what they tell me, they say it will probably be okay," she told him, staring at the good-looking blond boy with a detachment she had never before experienced in regard to Steve.

"Have you been okay up to now? I mean, at that Salvation Army place?"

Gail nodded, reaching for the remote control to turn the television off. "It's fine."

He shifted his weight from one foot to the other, glancing about the room.

"There's a chair," Gail finally offered. "You can sit down."

He shook his head. "I can't stay long."

"Oh. . . . " She wished he would leave then.

"I wanted to come tell you something," Steve spoke at last after a long silence. "I'll be going to Wyoming right after graduation this spring. Dad has an uncle who owns a ranch in the high desert near the Green River. I spent a summer with him and his family three years ago. It was different than anything I'd ever known. It's open and free with lots of space to think. I liked it.

"Anyway, I wrote and asked if he might have a job for me and he called and said he does. Their kids are all grown and gone. He said he could use some extra help. There's a little cabin on his place where I'll live, so I can be on my own. If everything works out I'll probably be there at least a year."

Gail registered surprise. "What about your plans to be a doctor? I thought you'd be going to college this fall."

He shook his head. "I couldn't hack it right now. Not after everything that's happened. I've got to get away and try to get hold of what's really important to me."

"But you told me you'd never change your plans. The baby has nothing to do with your future, you know. Not now."

Steve looked at her, his expression pained. "Do you honestly believe this baby, and everything that's happened, has had no affect on me? I've been dying inside. Little by little. That's *my* baby, too, you know."

She stared at him and then reached out a hand. He came closer and took it reluctantly. His expression clouded, as though he was going to cry. "Steve, I had no idea you felt this way. You never said a thing. I didn't think you cared."

"Didn't care...." His voice broke as he stepped back from the bed. "I've stayed home where I have everything, while you went away to some sort of strange institution to give our baby away to people we don't know anything about. Do you really believe I'm that shallow? Did you honestly think it would make no difference to me?"

She had been wrong about him. She could see that now. His seeming indifference had been a cover. Then, too, there had been the pressure from his mother. "How does your mother feel about your going to Wyoming instead of college?"

A smile relaxed his boyish face. "About the way you'd expect. After exploding, she tried every tactic she could come up with to change my mind. Dad finally told her to lay off. That was the first time I'd ever heard him come down on her like that."

Gail could not help smiling. "That's sort of what he did with her the night I walked to your place after seeing my mother."

Changing the subject, Steve asked, "Are you still going to give the baby up for adoption after it's born?"

"I'm not entirely sure. At times it seems the only thing to do. At other times I can't face the thought of giving it up. My mom asked me to bring it back home to her place, but I really don't think that would work out. I want to keep it but so far I haven't figured out how."

She wondered if she should tell him about his father's offer to adopt their child. Deciding she had nothing to lose, she added, "Did you know your father asked to adopt the baby?"

"Yeah, he told me. I was glad you turned him down. That wouldn't have worked either. Not the way Mom feels about everything."

Then he asked, "Gail, would you still like for us to get married for the baby's sake?"

"We don't love each other, Steve."

"But we both care about our baby."

She shook her head. "That's not enough. It's not enough to make a marriage work, especially when we're this young."

"We could at least give it a try. Getting married would give the baby a name. You could come with me to Wyoming."

"Do you love me, Steve?"

He hesitated before answering. "No, I guess I really don't."

Gail shook her head. "I need to be loved—by someone." She wanted to add that the Miller name did not thrill her all that much, but she controlled the urge.

Steve sighed. "Well, I wanted you to know what I was going to do, and that I was willing, in case you wanted to get married. I hate seeing you alone right now. Especially after all you've been through."

"I'm not alone, Steve. The home is filled with girls and babies."

They talked for a while and Steve told her more about his plans. He said he still thought he wanted to be a doctor someday. "But I need to get away first to do some serious growing up. Wyoming and the ranch seem like the place to do it."

He asked then what she was going to do after the baby arrived.

"I'm supposed to go to a new foster home. It will be hard, but easier I think than going back and having to face the kids at school. Knowing Lorna, it's probably all over the place by now."

Gail promised to let Steve know when their baby was born, and what she finally decided to do. When he left she lay there alone thinking. She had not realized how much his seeming indifference to her and their baby had hurt. Just knowing he cared— at least about their child— meant a great deal to her.

In one way she was sorry he had changed his plans about going on to college in the fall. Still, it really didn't seem fair for the father of her baby not to feel some of the hurt and disruption. A Wyoming ranch might be good for him, Gail decided. Away from Joanna he would be able to think through his future for himself, probably for the first time in his life.

She smiled there alone in the empty room. It was a relief being freed from the bitterness she had carried regarding Steve. A great relief!

14

God Cares

Gail returned to the home two days later, cautioned to rest when not attending class. She was released from dining room duty, and checked on by a nurse from the infirmary twice a day.

Joyce and her baby had been assigned to another room, for which Gail and her roommates were grateful. This did not, however, stop Joyce from dropping by with her infant sometimes several times a day. The birth of the delicate, tiny child had done nothing to soften its mother.

Janet finally had all of the pouty-mouthed blond she could handle. Blocking the doorway one evening as Joyce was about to walk on in, Janet announced, "The doctor says Gail has to avoid stress. And let's face it, Joyce, you're just about the most stressful person I've ever been around!"

Withdrawing without retort, Joyce was back again soon after Janet left to go to the sewing room.

A few days later a letter came from Terri offering Gail a glowing sense of having done something right as she waited out her final weeks. Terri's baby was by then nearly two months old. She wrote:

Dear Gail,

I'm so glad I decided to keep Jimmy. He's a doll. You had a lot to do with that decision, you know. Those times we talked and compared our lives and home situations helped me make up my mind when the time finally came.

Although it hasn't been easy coming back here with a baby. Some of the kids at school still make remarks. Most of our church friends were great. A few condemned us for keeping the baby, and me especially for getting pregnant in the first place. I was wrong getting so involved with Jimmy's father in that way, and I know it.

Dad went to our minister and asked if we as a family could dedicate Jimmy to the Lord. The minister agreed and so that's what we did last Sunday—Mom, Dad, my little brother, and me. We promised, before God and the congregation, we would raise Jimmy to love and know the Lord.

Gail, I was so scared standing up there holding Jimmy in front of all those people. Then all of a sudden I knew I had to say something.

I told them I had asked God's forgiveness, and need their forgiveness, too. As I stood there looking into their faces I saw tears in some of their eyes, even some of the men.

Afterward people came up to me. Some just gave me and Jimmy a hug, or said they loved us. Others told me they would be praying for us. Their forgiveness and acceptance of Jimmy and me helped. I don't need to go around feeling ashamed anymore. I can look people right in the eye now, and I do. After all, if the Lord can forgive me I should be able to forgive myself, don't you think?

I'm praying for you, Gail. My folks are, too. We pray you'll be able to do what's best for you and your baby when the time comes. I know your situation is different from mine. I'm praying, too, you'll decide you want to know the Lord. He's not only a powerful God, Gail, but the best and closest friend anyone could ever have.

May God bless you. Thank you again for helping me see beyond just me. I'll always be grateful. Jesus and I love you.

Your friend forever,
Terri

Terri's letter caused Gail to rethink her decision about going to a new foster home after the birth of her child. It wouldn't be easy going back to the Grants and Hillwood High School. Steve would be there for another couple of months. And yet, if Terri was able to return home to her school and church *with* her baby, maybe it would be possible to return to the Grants. Of course, they had not asked her lately. It had been her decision to leave. Maybe Sue and Mack didn't want her back. After all, there was still Ginger and the resentment that had wedged them apart.

At last Gail appeared to have passed the danger point of losing her baby. Mrs. Howard told her they would try to keep from assigning the fourth bed in her room until after she delivered. "We're afraid the pressure you've been under, first with Margo and then with Joyce, may have brought on the problem."

Denise remained subdued after Margo's baby died. It was as though a light had gone out of the twelve-year-old. Her former childlike belief, of everything turning out the way she dreamed, was gone. Denise was in fact bordering on severe depression as her baby's birth drew closer. Gail herself was miserable, both emotionally and physically. With the added body weight, and having to get up to go to the bathroom every little while all night long, she was never able to get much sleep.

Then one afternoon during the last week of March Gail came back to the room to find Denise huddled on her bed crying. "What's wrong?" Gail coaxed, sitting beside her.

155

"They've found out," Denise wailed. "Now Mom won't get my baby."

"Who found out?"

"The welfare people. Mom called and told me I'd talked too much about our plans. She said someone here must have told." The girl turned her head to look at Gail, tears streaking her face. "You didn't tell them, did you?"

Gail shook her head as she handed the girl a tissue. "I wouldn't do that."

Denise sat up and blew her nose. "The welfare people didn't know my dad was anywhere around. Now they're going to make him support us. Mom says Dad knows the baby is really mine now, and that she's not pregnant. He says he won't pay for my baby, and so I can't take it home with me after all."

The girl collapsed in tears again as Gail gathered Denise in her arms, cradling her like the child she was. "Maybe it will be better for everyone if you do relinquish your baby."

"But Mom wanted it."

"It's your baby, not your mother's. You have to think of what's best for you and the baby, not what your mother wants or doesn't want."

"I wanted to help take care of it. Now Mom's going to tell the neighbors she lost the baby she was supposed to be pregnant with so they won't know she lied. She's really mad at me.

Gail sighed. "At least she won't have to stuff her clothes with a pillow every morning." It had all seemed so ridiculous. "Does your father know where you are?"

"I don't know. Mom said the reason he left us was he'd lost his job and couldn't support us all. When he found another job he and Mom decided to keep on the way they were."

At last Denise cried herself to sleep. Gail pulled a pillow

under her head, covered the girl with a blanket, and then left to find Mrs. Howard. She told the woman about Denise's state of mind. "We'd better keep an eye on her," Gail cautioned.

Each day and night seemed longer than the one before as Gail and Denise maneuvered their out-of-balance bodies from place to place. Even getting up and down from a chair or a bed took considerable effort as the girls reached the last weeks of their pregnancies. Denise remained in a daze most of the time, unable to concentrate on her schoolwork, spending her free time in their room.

Gail was anxious to have her own pregnancy over with, and yet.... Her head told her she would sign the adoption papers when the time came, but her heart hung back from the decision.

Sue visited one afternoon telling Gail she had contacted the adoption agency, learning they had chosen a couple for Gail's baby. Sue assumed Gail still intended to relinquish her child. She had no idea of the doubts that continued to poke and nudge.

Up to that time Gail had not mentioned her plans to any of the girls but Terri. With Terri gone she felt the need to talk to someone. She chose Janet one evening as they stood alone at the end of the hallway together looking out over the lights of the city below.

"I haven't told Sue I'm having doubts. I suppose it's because deep down I know adoption is the only way out for me and my baby. Oh, Janet, how I dread it. Especially as the time gets closer. I also dread having to go to a new foster home. Sue hasn't said a thing for a couple of months about wanting me back."

"Have you considered keeping your baby and staying on here for a while?" the young black woman questioned. "It would give you more time to make up your mind.

Maybe you could work something out."

Gail shook her head. "No, I'd still be only sixteen when I had to leave. What would I have to offer a child?"

After a thoughtful silence, Janet noted, "I wish there was something I could do to help. But Gail, it's going to be rough for me, too, out there alone with a baby."

When they returned to the room they found Denise even more despondent. Gail was not only worried about the younger girl, but had to admit Janet had probably been right in warning her she might be jeopardizing her own baby by involving herself in Denise's problems. And yet, how could she avoid it?

That night Gail prayed for Denise and for herself. But she felt no better. She wasn't even sure God heard or cared. It was then she decided to call Pastor Wilkes. Maybe he could offer advise on how to help Denise. Or better yet, maybe he would talk to the girl.

She made the call right after breakfast. The minister told her he would come see her later that day. Gail halfheartedly protested, telling him he really didn't need to, and yet she was glad he was coming.

It was a sunlit early spring afternoon when Pastor Wilkes drove into the parking lot, his car tires crunching on the gravel scattered over the driveway. Gail had been hanging around the administration building waiting for him, after telling Mary Tripp he was coming to see her. It had rained that morning, but the clouds were at last billowing off toward the north, allowing the sun its turn to nourish the blossoming earth.

Gail met the pastor as he got out of his car. He wore a dark suit and tie, his wavy white hair fluffed out around his ears framing his gentle round face like a halo. Gail suggested they remain outside, leading the way to a ledge that overlooked the city.

He readily agreed. "It's too nice to be inside. I detected

a call for help when you phoned this morning," he said as they strolled along the paved walkway that edged the grounds. "Since two people canceled their appointments with me for this afternoon, it freed up the rest of my day."

"I'm glad," Gail replied. "A lot has happened and I'm not sure how to handle it." She stopped, turning to face the tall white-haired man. "I wanted to talk to you about Denise. And then there's still my own problem. My baby will be born any day and.... And I'm just not sure I can give it up."

He took Gail by the arm, leading her to a bench a few steps beyond. Below the hill through an opening in the trees the city spread out before them. Off to one side a gray squirrel scrambled up the side of a tree trunk to a low branch, then with a twitch of its thick tail leaped across to another branch and disappeared. On the lawn close by a robin carried on a wrestling match with a reluctant worm, forcing Gail to look the other way.

The man covered the girl's hand with his big one as they sat there. "Gail, I can well imagine the turmoil you must be feeling as your baby's birth draws closer."

She nodded then told him about Denise and all that had been happening. "I'd like to help her, but I don't know how. Maybe you could talk to her. It might help if you told her about Jesus. You know, some of those things you told me, about how Jesus loves us and all that. I'm afraid of what will happen if she isn't given something to hang onto."

"I don't think they'd let me see her unless she requested a visit. I can't just barge into a place like this. Why don't you tell her."

"Me?"

"Yes, you."

"But I don't know anything. What could I say that would help?"

He tilted his head to one side, then asked, "Gail, tell me about God. What do you think he's like?"

The question startled her. "You know more about that than I do."

"Well, what would you guess he's like? After all, neither of us have actually seen him. Give it a try. If you were to see God, what do you think he'd be like?"

"Boy!" She took in a lungful of sun-spiced air and slowly let it out. "Well.... He's probably big. Maybe like a giant. And he's old. He may be tired, too, especially if he made the world and everything, cause he's sure not keeping very good track of what's going on down here. Or maybe it's just because he lives a long ways away." She glanced at the minister, afraid he might be offended or even laugh.

When he spoke his voice was steady and low. "Then you see God as a tired old man who doesn't care very much about what happens to us."

"I guess maybe I do, although I've never put words to my thoughts before. I mean, if God really cared, would he stand by and let people kill one another, or starve to death, or not love their kids?" Gail could feel anger in her words.

Pastor Wilkes leaned back, the sun bathing his face. "Feel the sun, Gail? See the trees? You can actually smell the greening of spring."

"Yes. But...."

"Do you honestly believe God cares nothing about us when he's given us all these good things? When he holds everything together by his power. God's not the one who's forgotten us, Gail. We're the ones who've turned away. Why, his Spirit is here with us right this minute."

The thought of God's Spirit hanging around, listening to them talk made Gail squirm. "Then why does he let bad things happen to us?" A dry lump was forming in her throat. Choking it down she added, "Why did he let me get pregnant? And Denise? She's practically a baby yet herself."

"You and Denise made your own choices."

"But we didn't really understand. I mean, it's all turned out so different... What does God expect of us now, anyway?"

There was a tenderness in the man's gray eyes as his brow furrows deepened. "God expects you to look to him for help and guidance. He longs for a loving caring family, just as you have always longed for one. He sent his Son, Jesus, to gather a family for himself, a family of believers who will love him because they want to—not because they have to. If God zapped you every time you made a wrong move, you'd come to dread him. That's not the way a father wants his children to feel about him."

Gail sat there smothering for a time in her own brooding silence. "I used to long for my mother to love me like that. Just because she wanted to."

He nodded. "That's what God wants, Gail. He wants a close relationship with his people."

"How does a person get close to God? Maybe it would help Denise if I could tell her."

"You aren't interested for yourself?" he questioned.

"I suppose I could be. Someday."

"All right." He reached into his jacket pocket, pulling out a small leather-covered Bible. After reading several verses aloud he jotted the verse numbers on a note pad.

It was about the "Son of man" (the pastor explained this was Jesus) who was sent by God to be "lifted up" (as on the cross, said Pastor Wilkes, where Jesus died and again later when he was taken back to be with God). It told how the Son of God came so that the world "through him" could be saved. It was the last verse that struck Gail, the one that began, "Whoever believes in him [that meant

Jesus, according to Pastor Wilkes] is not condemned, but whoever does not believe is condemned already. . . ."

"I guess that's me," Gail remarked.

"It doesn't have to be," the pastor pointed out. "Not if you come to the place where you want God's love and forgiveness. Ask him to forgive you because of what Jesus did when he died for you on the cross. However," Pastor Wilkes's eyes registered a warning, "you need to mean business with God. He won't pay attention otherwise."

"Is that all there is to it?" she asked.

He smiled. "That's just the beginning. It opens the door to an exciting relationship that lasts beyond forever."

Now she was smiling. "That's a pretty long time. Remember, though, I wasn't asking for myself," she reminded, "but for Denise. Being a Christian sounds a little like Denise's happily-ever-after endings."

"Hardly!" Pastor Wilkes replied. "A Christian's life isn't without its bumps and bruises. We all face trials—the best and the worst of us. The difference is that Christians have the Lord to help them."

Before Pastor Wilkes left for the long drive home, he prayed with Gail, for her and Denise and the other young women there at the Salvation Army home. He mentioned their babies too, the ones already born and those waiting to be born. Then he handed Gail the list of Bible verses he had written down and showed her how to look them up.

"When you read those verses to Denise," he suggested, "why don't you concentrate on the book of John, chapter three, verses fourteen through eighteen. Go over them with her. And, Gail, don't forget to think about them yourself."

It was after dinner before Gail was finally able to talk to Denise. They were in their room alone. Denise was sitting by the window looking out at nothing in particular.

"How are you tonight?" Gail asked from where she sat across the room on her bed.

"I don't know," the younger girl replied in a monotone.

"I think I know," Gail told her. "We're both feeling lost and afraid. And alone."

Denise nodded then turned around. "You, too?"

"Yeah. But lately I've been more afraid for you than for me. I talked to my pastor about you today. I hope you don't mind. Actually I talked to him about both of us."

Lifting her shoulders in a half shrug, the girl responded, "Doesn't matter anymore."

"Pastor Wilkes told me how much God loves us. He said God cares about our babies, too."

"Why should God care now. He hasn't before."

"I believe he has, Denise. I believe he has—and does." Gail realized she *did* believe the words her ears heard her mouth uttering. "God *does* loves us. He really does." And the sound was good.

The younger girl's eyes widened. "He does? You really believe that?"

"Yeah. I really do. God cares. Why else would he send Jesus?"

"I learned about Jesus when I was a kid. I went to Sunday school for a while a couple years ago."

Gail reached for the Bible she kept in her desk drawer, then brought out the paper Pastor Wilkes had listed the Bible verses on. "Let's look these up together."

Denise came to sit beside Gail on the bed, her eyes eagerly following along as Gail read aloud. When Gail finished, Denise began yanking on her arm. "Let's do it! You and me. Right now. Okay?"

"Do what?" Gail asked grasping the girl's wrist to keep from being pulled off balance.

"Let's tell God we're sorry and that we love him. Please, Gail. Let's do it together now."

"I-I can't. I mean, not just yet. I need time. It's not something you rush into."

"Why not? I want to. Right now."

Slowly Gail closed the Bible. A part of her wanted to, and yet Pastor Wilkes had said God would know if she didn't mean it. She just wasn't sure she was ready. "Denise, why don't you go find Mrs. Howard. I'm pretty sure she's a Christian. She can help you a lot better than me. I need to think about it a little more. Okay?"

Before Gail could utter another word, Denise was up and out the door.

"Oh.... Wow!" Gail breathed aloud to the now empty room. "I guess she was ready all right. I wish..." Lifting her face, Gail closed her eyes as a deep sadness came over her. "I wish I could be that open to you, God. I wish it was me."

She started to put her Bible back in the drawer, then decided to leave it out. Maybe she would try reading it later. Or maybe Denise would want to. She wondered why she was so hesitant about approaching God. Was she afraid He wouldn't accept her? She didn't think she could stand being rejected again right then. Especially by God.

During the next few days Gail watched Denise's depression slowly heal. The younger girl noted one evening, "It's like God is deep inside someplace soothing the sadness that's still in there hurting for my baby."

Gail was relieved the worst of the younger girl's depression had passed. She wished she was as ready to step away from herself and reach out to God.

But she wasn't. Not yet.

15

Decision Time

And then it was mid April—exactly one week from Gail's due date.

Denise, her baby expected a few days later than Gail's, was slowly recovering from the blow of not being able to take her child home to her mother. The younger girl had at last faced the reality of giving her baby up. She was beginning to look forward to returning to her family, while continuing to spend time with Mrs. Howard learning more about God from the Bible. Gail didn't know if that was the reason for Denise's developing confidence in the future or not, but the girl had obviously found something to hold onto.

Would she—herself—Gail wondered, ever again come as close to accepting God as that night when she sent Denise off alone to find Mrs. Howard? Gail had been poised right on the edge of reaching out to the Lord, only to pull back, too frightened to let go. She had not been sure enough of him or of herself to take the chance.

Joyce was at last leaving Gail and her roommates alone after attaching herself to a couple of girls downstairs. Joyce's neglect of her tiny daughter, now a month old, was the talk of the dorm.

"If it weren't for her roommate," Janet remarked one morning during breakfast, "I don't know what would become of that baby."

"How come the social services people don't take the baby away from her?" Gail wondered aloud, chasing a last forkful of scrambled egg around her plate.

Janet was staring across the dining room to where Joyce sat laughing with her new huddle of friends. "If she doesn't pull her act together soon, they may have to."

After shunning their company for days, Joyce unexpectedly appeared that night at their door. Janet was lying on the bed reading while Denise sat at her desk, hunched uncomfortably over her round stomach, homework spread out before her. Gail had propped herself against the head of her bed with a pillow, intent on writing a letter to Terri. The three looked up when Joyce opened the door without knocking.

"I came to say farewell," Joyce breezed. "I'm leaving this rat trap tonight. I've had all the rules and hassle I can take."

Her pen poised over the letter, Gail asked, "Are you going home?"

"In a week. Some of my friends from school are out for spring vacation. They're coming by to take me with them. I talked to my folks and they gave their permission as long as I go home and back to school when the week's over."

"You've got to be kidding!" Janet declared, closing her book over a thumb as she sat up. "Your parents are actually letting you go off like that with a bunch of high school kids? And with a baby?"

"I'm not taking her," Joyce announced. "I signed adoption papers awhile ago. They've already come and taken her away."

"You've given your baby up after having her for a whole month?" Denise turned pale. "How could you do it?"

Joyce shrugged. "I'm too young to raise a kid. I want to have fun. . . . You know, do things. Taking care of a baby is a drag. And besides, it's better for her this way."

"You bet it is!" Janet remarked.

Gail wordlessly agreed. It would be far better for Joyce's baby.

"Well, just thought I'd stop to say good-bye to all you inmates and wish you luck when your time comes." With that Joyce turned to leave.

"Yeah, you too," Gail called after her.

"The only luck she'll be able to dredge up is found under a rock," Janet remarked as the door closed behind the bleached blonde.

Gail sighed audibly. "There goes trouble."

Janet nodded, flipping her book open with a snap. "At least it won't touch her baby now."

"How can Joyce give her baby away after having her all this time?" Denise inquired again, her voice raw with disbelief.

Neither Gail nor Janet replied. They had no explanation for Joyce's erratic actions.

Gail's due date passed with no indication her baby was about to put in an appearance. Her hospital bag had been packed for the last three weeks, her letter and Steve's to their unborn child tucked into a side pocket.

She had heard nothing from Steve since he visited her at the hospital. But then, she hadn't expected to. After writing to her mother a couple of times, she finally gave that up as a lost cause. Gail reasoned if her mother meant the things she had said about changing her lifestyle, she would have stayed in touch to prove her sincerity. At the very least she would have answered Gail's letters. While Gail tried to put her mother's offer, as well as Steve's, out of her mind as completely unworkable, she could not help wondering about what might have been. Both offers would let her keep her baby. Had she been too hasty in turning down one or the other of them?

On Sue's last visit Ginger had come with her mother. Since Gail had no chance for seclusion living at the home she had learned to communicate better with those around her. Because of that Gail found talking with Ginger easier now. Both appeared to have passed the point of merely tolerating one another. Gail detected a mellowing in the redhead. But then, she admitted she had done some mellowing herself.

Two nights after Sue's last visit, the end of Gail's nine months of waiting, tears, and dashed dreams came crashing in on her without warning. She had gone to bed early, tired beyond reason, but could not fall asleep. No matter which way she turned, or how many times she plumped her pillow, sleep flitted just beyond reach. During those wakeful hours, while the others slept, Gail's mind darted in one direction and then another, seeking an avenue of escape with her baby. The dark silence of night hovered over her with its own brand of ominous despair as she sought a way to keep her baby. Finally she grew sick of thinking about it.

Rising from her bed in the hushed stillness of the night, Gail went out to walk the hall alone, padding up and down the cold tile floor in her bare feet. She counted the squares to focus her mind on something. There were eighty-six tiles up and eighty-six tiles back. It was nearly two in the morning when she finally returned to her room, quietly easing her bulk back into bed to at last fall away to a fitful sleep.

She awoke an hour later as a mild pain sliced across her midsection wrapping itself around to her lower back. It was starting. . . . Soon her baby would cease being an "It," born with an identity of his or her own. Gail lay there for an hour as the pains grew closer together. She gripped the blanket and held on as a contraction stabbed at her only to flee again.

Remembering Margo, and how she had waited too long, Gail finally got up and woke Janet. "I think you'd better go call someone," she whispered close to the sleepy black girl's ear.

Denise awoke when the light came on, sitting with Gail while Janet went for help. "I'll be praying for you," Denise assured her. "The Lord won't let anything bad happen to you or your baby. I just know it."

An ambulance arrived, roaring Gail off to the hospital. Once there the chain of activity kept her mind from probing the future. She was placed in a small cubicle and examined by an intern. "It won't be long," he told her. "Looks as though this is going to be a short labor. You're a lucky young lady. Most first-time mothers take hours to give birth."

Lucky? Gail would have laughed if she hadn't been so scared. She felt anything but lucky. The pain would not have been nearly so difficult to endure if she knew that at the end of it she could keep her baby.

A thickset middle-aged nurse scuffed into the room to inquire what type of childbirth Gail had decided upon. Lines of fatigue sagged the woman's florid face.

"I don't care," Gail told her, "as long as I don't see the baby. Please. . . . Don't let me see it."

The woman turned without comment, giving orders to a younger nurse who had just bustled in. Gail clinched her fists against the next pain as it shot through her. The second nurse moved to Gail's side cautioning her to relax. Gail began taking short panting breaths as she had learned during childbirth classes at the home.

Time passed with no sense of beginning or end. It was pain, pant, relax.... Over and over, again and again the contractions bore down until they were coming so close there seemed hardly any space between. She asked how long she had been there. Only three hours? It seemed forever. Why did it have to hurt like this?

She tried again to pray, but could only get to, "Oh, God...." before another stab tore into her. The one that followed was even sharper. Gail screamed.

Both nurses rushed back to her side. The heavy one examined Gail then called for the intern to help boost her onto a gurney. "Doctor's on his way," the younger nurse told Gail as they wheeled her off to the delivery room.

Gail reached out, gripping the intern's arm. "It's nearly here, isn't it?"

He nodded. "Won't be much longer."

She twisted her head so she could see the older nurse. "You won't let me see the baby will you?"

"You don't have to see it," the woman assured her. "Now try to relax."

The delivery table that they slid her onto was cold. There was flurry of activity as two other nurses came in dressed in sea-green cover-ups, complete with surgical masks. Gail recognized the doctor's voice then. She looked up to find him standing over her. A bright overhead light was switched on, beamed toward the table where she lay. Panic shattered her. It was too light! Way too light! She would see the baby. She didn't want to see it if she couldn't keep it.

"Please! I want to go to sleep now," she begged, crying out as a searing pain hit again, pressing her hard against the table.

Someone had hold of an ankle. Her knee was bent and

her foot placed in a side stirrup. The other leg was positioned and the sheet cupped in.

The doctor patted her arm. "Don't fight it, Gail. You're doing just fine."

"I don't want to see it," Gail gasp. "I have to give my baby away. Doesn't anyone understand?"

"Yes, yes, Gail. All right now. We're ready. Bear down hard. Give it all you've got with the next contraction." It was the doctor talking again.

She did as told. She couldn't have stopped if she had wanted to. Her whole body bore the pressure. She felt dazed.

When she rallied again the awful intense pain was gone. Opening her eyes she noticed the bright light had been turned off. She was still on the delivery table, but the doctor was gone. Only two nurses remained in the room, pans and instruments clinking as they worked. One was the heavy middle-aged nurse from the labor room. It was as though Gail had been cast off on an island, left behind as the ship sailed on without her.

"My baby?" she managed to whisper.

The nurse glanced at her. "It's over, honey. The baby's in the nursery. It's fine and so are you."

"What is it? The baby, I mean."

The woman came to Gail's side, the heels of her run-over shoes dragging. She placed a hand on the girl's forehead, brushing the dark hair back from her face. "I thought you didn't want to know."

Gail shook her head. "I said I didn't want to see it. But I do want to know. Is it a girl or a boy?"

"You sure about that?" the nurse persisted. "Some girls who relinquish don't even want to know the sex."

"Well, I do," Gail responded.

"All right. You had a girl. Eight pounds, four ounces."

Gail sighed. A girl. . . .

She was moved to a private room previously arranged for by Dr. Miller. Exhausted, Gail fell asleep as soon as the nurse left her room.

When she awoke Sue was sitting beside her bed, a vase of tiny yellow rose buds on the stand beside her. "From the three Grants," Sue spoke, reaching for Gail's hand. "How are you?"

Gail stretched. "All right, I guess. Did they call you?" She ran a hand over her stomach. It was still swollen, but not as before. It seemed odd, being separated from her child after all these months.

"I left word to have them call me the minute you were brought to the hospital. I woke Ginger and told her to get in touch with my boss when she got up so he'd know I wouldn't be in today. Then I started driving. I got here just before the baby was born."

"Did they tell you I had a girl?"

Sue nodded. "I saw her."

Gail's dark eyes widened as she pushed a tangle of hair back her cheek. "You did? What's she like?"

"She's pretty. Prettiest baby in the nursery. Looks a lot like her mother, I think. She has fuzzy dark hair and tiny full lips."

Gail smiled. "Good. At least she doesn't look like Joanna Miller. Does Steve know she's here?"

"Ginger will probably tell him you started labor if she sees him at school. Would you like me to call him when I get home?"

"Please. I told him I'd let him know."

"Ginger talked to Steve the other day. He told her you weren't sure about putting the baby up for adoption when he saw you last month. I've been under the impression you had your mind made up before you left for the Salvation Army home. Steve's going to want to know what you've decided."

"I guess I should have told you I was having doubts," Gail spoke apologetically. "First I'm sure I'll sign the papers, then I don't see how I can. I'm so mixed up."

"You've already signed the preliminary papers," Sue reminded.

"I know. But they told me it wouldn't be final until after the baby was born and I'd signed the papers their attorney brought to the hospital. Even then there's supposed to be a waiting period before it's final."

"It wouldn't be fair to the people who took your baby if you backed down later and tried to take her away from them," Sue pointed out. "Especially if they'd had her awhile."

"I know." Gail turned on her side facing Sue. Her body was sore and stiff. "Remember the letters Steve and I wrote? No one's ever said whether or not the adoptive parents agreed to give them to her when she gets older. I want to make sure she reads those letters someday. I think I'd like to know something about the couple who want her, too."

Things were clarifying in Gail's mind as she spoke. "I won't sign any more papers until I know my daughter ..." Her voice caught in mid-sentence. "Until I know she'll get to read those letters, and I find out what the adoptive parents are like." It sounded so strange. All her life Gail had *been* a daughter. Now she *had* a daughter.

Sue studied Gail thoughtfully. "I'd feel the same if I were you. I'll go call the agency right now. I'll remind them of the letters as well as your request to know something about the couple."

Sue left the room, returning a few minutes later. "I talked to a Mr. Brant, the attorney for the adoption agency. I told him you wanted to meet the couple. I also reminded him of the letters. He's going to ask them to come see you."

"You mean I'd actually meet them? Talk to them?" Gail pulled herself up on an elbow. "I don't know. . . ."

Appearing satisfied with herself, Sue said, "I also told him he'd better write something into the adoption agreement about the child being given those letters when she's older. He didn't much like that. But when I told him those were your conditions, he said he would. He's bringing the papers by this evening for you to sign."

Smiling, Gail lay back. "Sounds like you really did tell him. You know, I think I would like to meet them—the people who want my baby, I mean. Maybe it will help me decide what to do." She added, "But I'm not promising to give her up yet."

Sue dampened a cloth so Gail could wash her hands and face. Then picking up a hair brush, the woman gently began brushing the girl's hair, fanning the dark locks out over the pillow.

After lunch Gail dozed off and on while Sue sat quietly by reading. The phone rang once. It was Pastor Wilkes. He said Ginger had just called him. A short time later a pot of red tulips was delivered from the church.

It was late afternoon when Sue left. "I'll be here in the morning before they take you back to the infirmary." she promised.

Shortly after Gail's dinner tray was taken away, a tall heavy jowled man in a wrinkled gray business suit walked into her room carrying a briefcase. He introduced himself as Jaimison Brant, handing her a card with his name imprinted on it. Gail wondered if he was trying to impress or intimidate her as he stood close to the bed, towering above her.

"The adoptive couple are here," he announced in a brusque tone. "They just flew in. Personally, I don't like the idea. But they're willing to meet with you.

"Mrs. Grant told me you're having second thoughts

about letting the baby go. I had been under the impression you'd made up your mind when you first went to the adoption agency I represent." He braced a hand on the overhead bar. "You should realize, young lady, these people have been counting on this baby for months. It would be heartless to take it away from them now. They've been waiting to adopt for nearly five years."

Scooting herself to an upright position, Gail glared up at the man, her mouth in a full pout. "She's still my baby! So don't talk to me about being heartless."

The man just stood there staring at her, returning her glowering glare. "Do you still want to see them?"

"Yes. Alone," she snapped.

He turned abruptly and left, as Gail's anger changed to fear. They were actually here.... At the hospital. The man and woman who wanted her daughter. A chill of reality clinched its cold fingers around her as a knock thumped at the door.

Stiff with apprehension, Gail called out, "Come in."

The door opened and a man and woman in their mid-thirties entered. The woman was a willowy clear-faced Scandinavian-type with sandy shoulder length hair. The man was a little taller, with a shock of unruly dark hair above penetrating blue eyes.

"Hello, Gail." The man appeared ill at ease as he stepped ahead of his wife who had stopped at the foot of Gail's bed. "Mr. Brant cautioned us about disclosing our last names. I suppose it's best that way. My first name is Jim. My wife here is Kathy." He made an attempt to smile, but the effort was weak and strained.

Gail responded with a slight nod. He was scared. She hadn't thought of how they might be feeling.

Kathy moved closer. "I understand you'd like to know something about us before signing the adoption papers. I've been thinking about it. At first it frightened me. But

I've come to the conclusion that I'd want to know if I were in your place."

His hand on his wife's shoulder, Jim said, "We just saw the baby. She's a little beauty! I respect your protection of her."

"I haven't seen her. But I'm still not sure I can sign her away," Gail admitted. "I don't know what to do."

"We understand, Gail," Kathy conveyed. "Mr. Brant mentioned something about some letters you want her to have when she older. He's never mentioned letters to us before. Can you tell us what you have in mind?"

"He was supposed to have told you." Pointing to the closet, Gail said, "They're in my suitcase. I'd like you to read them."

Kathy found the letters and she and Jim read them in silence. When finished there were tears in Kathy's eyes. "Your love for that baby is embodied here on paper, Gail. I've wanted a child so desperately. And yet, right now, after reading your letter as well as the father's, I'd give anything if you two could keep her."

Appearing equally touched by what he had read, Jim asked, "What is it you want us to do with these?" Quickly he added, "That is, if you do decide to let us have her."

"Did you intend to tell her she was adopted?" Gail inquired.

"Yes," said Jim. "We've discussed that. We believe an adopted child should know right from the beginning so she never faces a sudden jolt concerning her parentage."

"Then all I ask is that you give her those letters when she's older, when she questions why her real mother and father gave her up. I'll sign no papers that don't include that agreement."

"I could consent to that," said Kathy, glancing at her husband.

Jim stood there for a quiet moment, then nodded. "I

think it would help her to know her natural parents cared." He held his empty hands in front of him, then let them fall to his side. "We already love that tiny little girl. We love her so much that, like you, we want only what's best for her."

Gail knew he meant it. He and Kathy had evidently been planning on this baby for months ... years. Five years, the attorney had said. Five years ago she had only been ten years old.

"You can ask Mr. Brant to come back in," Gail said, barely above a whisper. "Tell him to give me a few minutes alone first, though." She turned toward the wall as they left her room.

It was then she cried.

16

Family Strength

Gail slipped out of bed and into the new beige robe Sue and Mack had given her for her hospital stay. She had no idea she would be so weak. Carefully she made her way to the bathroom. It felt good having her face washed, and her teeth and hair brushed.

She was standing back by the foot of the bed at a window overlooking the parking lot when a nurse came in. "How are the sea legs? We don't want you falling or passing out on us now."

"It's good to be up."

"How would you like to take a wheelchair ride down the hall?" the nurse asked. "A girl from the Salvation Army home was just brought in. She's been asking to see you."

"Denise?"

"That's her. What a young one. Do you feel up to going down there for a couple of minutes?"

"Sure. But I can walk." She very much wanted to see

Denise. Besides, it would put off having to face Mr. Brant for a while.

Together they went out to the hall. Gail stopped and looked in both directions, but saw no sign of the man. She walked with the nurse toward the opposite end of the floor.

Denise was lying on a high narrow bed watching the door, smiling as bright as always when she saw Gail. "I was hoping you could come," Denise greeted her former roommate as the nurse pushed a chair beside the bed for Gail.

"Is the pain bad yet?" Gail asked as she sat down.

Denise bit at her upper lip. "At times. Did you watch your baby being born? They asked if I wanted to, but I told them I wasn't sure. I thought I did before. . . . I mean, when I was going to get to keep it. But now I don't know." The girl reached for Gail's hand and hung on as a contraction came and went. Once it passed, she asked, "Tell me, what should I do, Gail?"

"I can't tell you what to do. I can only tell you what I did."

"What?" Denise persisted, her eyes pleading.

"I told them I didn't want to see the baby." Gail stopped, then plunged on with the rest of it. "I'm giving her up, Denise." *There.* She had said it. Out loud. That made it more real.

"Then I'm going to tell them I don't want to see mine. I hope I grow up to be strong like you, Gail."

"I'm not any more grown up than you, Denise. And I'm sure far from strong."

"You don't ever want to see your baby then? Not ever?"

"Well. . . ." Gail grew thoughtful. "It might be good to see her. Just once. But I couldn't hold her or anything like that. It would be too hard."

Denise nodded. "Yeah. Way too hard. . . . I prayed for

you all night after they brought you here. Will you be praying for me?"

Taking Denise's hand, Gail squeezed it in silence. How could she pray for Denise when she hadn't been able to pray for herself? "I'll try."

"Promise?"

Gail nodded. "Promise."

The nurse came then and walked Gail back to her room. When they entered they found Mr. Brant waiting for them.

"I'd like to sit in a chair for a while," Gail told the nurse.

The attorney waited until the nurse left then asked abruptly, "Have you come to a decision? Jim told me I shouldn't pressure you. I hope you don't feel that I have."

Gail ignored his remark, asking, "Did you write about the letters in the adoption papers?"

"Yes." He took several sheets from his briefcase and handed them to her. "There on page two. I've marked the paragraph."

Securing her robe over her knees, Gail took the papers and began to read. Although there was another chair in the room, the man continued to stand. She ignored him. Most of what she read refused to sink in. She could see, however, the matter of the letters had been added. It stated that by the time the child reached her twenty-first birthday she was to have been given two letters written before her birth by her natural mother and father.

While Gail was not at all sure she could trust Mr. Brant, she felt she could trust Jim and Kathy. "Where do I sign?" she asked at last.

The man called the nurse back in to witness Gail's signature. Then with the adoption agreement safely in his brief case, the attorney left, a satisfied smile playing with the corners of his mouth.

A couple of minutes later Jim and Kathy came in.

Gail wiped at her eyes and attempted a smile. "She's yours now."

Kathy was shaking her head. "No, Gail. She's ours. Yours, mine, and Jim's."

"When are you taking her?"

"Tomorrow morning," Jim replied, the intense blue of his eyes betraying his anticipation.

"I go back to the home in the morning," Gail spoke to no one in particular. "I've been thinking. . . . I'd really like to see her. Just once."

Jim appeared dubious, but Kathy seemed to understand. "Tell you what," she said, "we'll come here to your room first thing in the morning. Then we can go down to the nursery window together."

"I'd like that."

Kathy suddenly knelt in front of Gail and put her arms around the girl. "Oh, Gail. We'll forever be grateful to you for giving us this child. For giving her birth. I'll love her for you and me both."

The two left as Gail's dinner tray was brought in. She got back into bed to eat, switching the overhead television on for company and something to focus her mind on. She was surprised to find she was hungry.

When the nurse returned for the tray Gail asked about Denise, learning the girl was progressing well. Turning the television and light off Gail lay there alone listening to the muffled hospital night noises. Visiting hours were over and she could see through the half-open door the hall lights had been dimmed. She thought about her baby just a few steps away from her. Would they ever again be this close?

To turn her mind off she tried approaching God about Denise. "She's so young," Gail whispered toward the darkened ceiling. "She's one of yours now, God. Please help her and her baby. I guess I don't have the right to ask you anything, but maybe you'll listen if it's for Denise."

She lay there, her mind in suspension. "I'd give anything if you'd forgive me for turning away from you—from your Son Jesus. I'm ready now, I think, to let go of whatever's been holding me back. You're sure not going to be getting much if you do accept me, though. . . . "

That was the last she remembered until she opened her eyes the next morning. She couldn't believe it. She had actually slept all night.

After a sponge bath and breakfast, Jim and Kathy came in. "We haven't seen the baby yet this morning," Jim said. "Thought we'd wait for you."

"That is," Kathy put in, "if you still want to do this."

The girl nodded, reaching for her robe. "I want to."

Gail held back, walking slower as they neared the nursery window. There were mixed feelings tumbling through her mind. Would this help, or make it harder? They turned a corner and there in front of them was the nursery. Small transparent bassinets lined the room, most of them occupied by sleeping infants. One was red faced, going through all the crying motions although hardly any sound reached them outside the thick glass.

Pointing to a bassinet near the window Jim, with a noticeable catch to his voice, said, "There—there she is."

Moving closer to the glass Gail stood looking in at the baby who had developed into a human being while inside her body during the last nine months. A rush of realization struck. That perfectly formed pink-skinned child might have been torn apart by an abortionist's tool, pieces of the tiny body tossed away as refuse. The vivid picture that flashed to her mind struck with such force she had to put her hand on the glass to steady herself.

"Are you all right?" Jim asked. "I can go find a wheelchair."

Gail was shaking her head. "I'll be okay."

The baby's full-formed lips were making sleepy sucking motions. While most of the other newborns had roundish faces, her baby's face was a perfect oval like, Gail realized, her own. The dark fuzz that would be hair had been brushed into a top curl. She stretched as the three watched from the opposite side of the glass, opened an eye, then relaxed, and drifted off to sleep again.

Gail watched in complete wonderment. "She's so small. And yet so. . . . So perfect. It's hard to fathom."

Kathy nodded and slipped an arm around her child's mother as Gail commented, "Some people wanted me to have an abortion, but I just couldn't. I'm so glad now!"

"So are we!" Jim responded. "So are we. You should be proud of what you've done by carrying this baby to term."

"I am," Gail told him. She smiled then. "I really am. And I don't feel a claim on her the way I thought I would. Getting pregnant was wrong, but giving this baby life was not. Maybe that helps offset the other a little.

"She doesn't belong to me. She belongs to herself—and to God. Even though you two are going to be her parents, she doesn't really belong to you either."

"We understand that, Gail," Kathy assured her. "We feel the same about the Lord. Your child will be raised as a Christian, knowing what the Lord—and you—have done for her."

"That's good," Gail responded, realizing Kathy was taking it for granted she was a Christian. Remembering her prayer of the night before, she decided she would call Pastor Wilkes as soon as possible to get that matter taken care of.

"Did you have any names in mind while you were carrying her?" Kathy asked.

Gail shook her head.

Glancing at his wife, Jim said, "We were going through

a book of names just this morning. We finally came across one we both liked. What do you think of Abigail for a first name?"

"Abigail?" Gail spoke thoughtfully. "It has part of my name in it. And yet it sounds more old-fashioned. I like it."

"Then it's settled," said Kathy. "Her name is Abigail."

"Do you have a middle name?" Jim asked.

"It's Marie."

"How does Abigail Marie strike the two of you?"

Kathy was nodding. "I love it."

Turning for one last look at the infant, Gail spoke, "You're going to have to love little Abigail for me."

We will," Jim told her as Kathy nodded.

"You don't have to go back to the room with me. Stay here with your baby. It's where you belong now."

With that Gail turned and walked away from the child, leaving tiny Abigail with her new father and mother. A heavy crushing sensation walked with her. And yet there were no regrets about her decision. It had been right. She had first given little Abigail Marie life—this child who would always bear her name—and now she had given her a family. Yes, the decision had been right.

An hour later, after being told Denise had just given birth to a healthy boy, Gail dressed for her return to the home's infirmary. She was sitting on the bed when the door opened and Sue, Mack, and Ginger walked in. She was surprised, since it was a weekday when Sue and Mack were usually at work and Ginger at school.

Sue rushed in breathless. "We were afraid you might have left already—before we could get here. We all three took the day off so we could come see you."

"We saw the baby and met the couple who are adopting her," Mack told Gail as he grabbed the startled girl up in a quick hug. "I'm so proud of you, kiddo!"

Gail glanced at Ginger over Mack's shoulder, wondering if the old jealousy would reappear. But the girl who had hung back when they first entered the room, was grinning.

"Hi," Ginger greeted her.

Gail smiled at the redhead. "Did you see Abigail Marie?"

"Abigail who?"

"The baby. That's what we named her. Jim, Kathy, and me."

"Oh.... Yeah, I saw her. She's pretty. Like," Ginger stopped and smiled again, "like you."

Gail blushed then told them about meeting Jim and Kathy and signing the adoption papers. She told them too about going to see the baby and how they had arrived at a name. "It hurts, letting her go like this," she added. "But not nearly as much as I thought it would." It wasn't easy, putting words to her feelings. "It hurts. But it seems right, too, letting Kathy and Jim have her. I've done at least one thing right. Maybe *that's* what feels good about it."

"We all, at some point in our lives, have to give our children up," Sue remarked. "Whether it's when they go off to college, get married, or just when they grow up and move out."

Gail agreed with a nod. "It gives me kind of an empty feeling." She glanced down at her stomach and laughed. It was good to laugh again. "In more ways than one!"

Ginger came closer. "What are you going to do now?"

"They're taking me back to the home for a week or so, then I suppose I'll be going to another foster home somewhere."

"I'd like it if ... I mean, we'd like it if you'd come back with us. Mom talked to them at the social services office and they said you can come live with us again if you want to. I just wanted you to know I'd like you to come back with us. We all would."

"You would? I didn't think you would after all that's happened."

"I've always wanted a sister. I guess I didn't know how to be one, though. If you'll come back home with us I promise to try harder. I'm not saying we'll never fight. But then most sisters do, I guess."

Gail looked at Mack and Sue. "Is this for real? You really want me to live with you again?"

"We really want you, Gail," Sue said as Mack exaggerated a nod.

"What about the kids at school? And Steve? What will the people at your church say?"

"We've talked it over," said Sue. "It's not going to be easy. But together as a family, we'll see it through. You'll have the three of us, as well as Pastor Wilkes, standing with you."

Smiling, Gail noted, "I've learned a lot at the home about getting along with people. I didn't make it easy on you before. I'm sorry about that."

"You'll come then?" Ginger prodded.

Glancing at Sue and Mack, then back to Ginger, Gail felt her emptiness filling with a warm glow from this family who wanted her as one of them again. "If you're sure you don't mind sharing your mom and dad with me?"

Ginger eyed her parents. "Oh, I think there's probably enough parental stewing on their part to include us both."

Slipping her arm around Ginger, Sue remarked, "I have a feeling there's something really fine in store for you, Gail, after all you've been through. As I've told you, I've been praying."

Mack nudged his wife. "Hey, *we've* been praying."

"But," Gail questioned, "are you sure God's been listening?"

"I know he has," Sue replied. "He's given you back to us, hasn't he?"

Gail turned on her serious expression. "Really? You mean it wasn't my decision after all?"

"Hey, don't underestimate Mom's praying," Ginger spoke up. "She's been praying up a storm about me lately, and...." The girl's impishness returned, "Just look at me! I'm becoming a regular nice-type."

Mack groaned and made a grab for his daughter, missing when Ginger sidestepped his reach. Gail laughed. And again it felt good.

When the minor bedlam quieted, Gail looked from Sue to Mack. "I'll never underestimate anything about any of you or your God, again. But I do have a condition."

"And that is...?" Sue inquired.

"If I go back to being your foster daughter," Gail glanced quickly toward Ginger, "and your foster sister, will someone, please, sit me down and not let me up until this Christian stuff comes clear to me? Last night I prayed and told God I wanted his forgiveness. But I'm not sure I got through to him.

"Be glad to," said Mack.

"I'll do my best," responded Sue at the same time, giving her husband a smiling sidelong glance.

"Oh, no!" Ginger declared, stepping in front of them both. "If Gail's going to be my sister, then I'm the one who gets to knock some sense into her hard head." Ginger winked at Gail with her back to her parents.

"Ginger!" Sue's voice registered shock at her daughter's choice of words.

Gail frowned. "Ginger may have a point. I mean, besides on the top of her head. After all, it probably takes a hard head to get through to one."

"Are you insinuating I'm a cone head?" Ginger demanded.

Sue stepped between the two. "Girls, girls. This is no way to...."

She stopped as the two burst out laughing. "Throwing her hands into the air, Sue turned back to Mack. "Just what are we letting ourselves in for here?"

Mack put his arm around his wife. "A family, Sue. Just a run of the mill, up and down, good times and bad times family."

Gail sat back on the bed, looking at her new family. Both she and her baby had families now. "I think I'll talk to Pastor Wilkes instead," Gail said with a smile.

[THE END]

The Author

Shirlee Evans began writing for Christian magazines while her two sons were growing up. A year after her first novel, *Robin and the Lovable Bronc*, was published (Moody Press, 1974), she went to work as a reporter and columnist for the Post Publications of Camas, Washington, a local weekly newspaper. During her first year there she received a Washington State Sigma Delta Chi award for investigative reporting. She did free-lance writing for the *Oregon Journal* (a large Portland, Oregon, daily which has since been taken over by *The Oregonian*).

On assignment for the *Oregon Journal*, Shirlee covered a junior high school's four-day abortion seminar. Intrigued with the reaction of the students—who recoiled at the thought of abortion—Shirlee did further research toward a fictionalized account of a pregnant teen. And so *A Life in Her Hands* came to be written.

Shirlee is author of three children's novels on the Oregon Coastal Indians in the mid 1800s, published by Herald Press. They are *Tree Tall and the Whiteskins*, 1985; *Tree Tall and the Horse Race*, 1986; and *Tree Tall to the Rescue*, 1987.

Shirlee left newspaper writing in 1981 to pursue her book projects. She works now for Kris' Hallmark Shop at Vancouver Mall, still managing to write up to five hours a day.

Born near Centralia, Washington, Shirlee and her husband, Bob, have lived north of Vancouver, Washington, near Battle Ground for most of their married lives. They have two sons, two "special" daughters-in-law, and six grandchildren. Shirlee attends Brush Prairie Conservative Baptist Church where she has been a member for over twenty years.